"How do you know me?"

"Who in Italy doesn't know the famous and beautiful Signora Ferrari of Massimo Domingo Art Detective Agency?"

"I wasn't aware anyone knew my name. My boss is the premier art expert."

"Signora, you're too modest. Your reputation precedes you, as does the highly questionable and fading reputation of your boss. And your particular expertise will be put to very good use here, I assure you. It's a special job that requires your particular skills."

"What exactly are we doing here?" Hadley demanded, acting more courageous than she felt.

"Okay, let's dispense with the niceties, if we must. I have inherited a number of paintings, and I'm in need of your talent in authenticating and tracking the provenance of what I believe are masterworks."

"You mean stolen Nazi art."

The man straightened. "Certainly not. I have the records that maintain these paintings were legally sold to the buyers and that I now own Palazzo Allegretti and all of its contents."

"But I understood that Herr Muller had purchased the palazzo."

"Herr Muller works for us. He's what you could call an anonymous third party. We've been waiting a long time to release these paintings onto the open market. I simply need your assistance in verifying their authenticity, perhaps giving us an idea of their current value, which has undoubtedly risen since they were…"

"Confiscated?" Hadley posed. "Is that the word you were looking for?"

To Nancy,

The Case
of the
Forgotten Fragonard

by

Marilyn Baron

A Massimo Domingo Mystery
Book 3

Thank you for your friendship and support.
Marilyn Baron

The Case of the Forgotten Fragonard

Cover Art by *The Wild Rose Press, Inc.*

The Wild Rose Press, Inc.
PO Box 708
Adams Basin, NY 14410-0708
Visit us at www.thewildrosepress.com

Publishing History
First Edition, 2022
Trade Paperback ISBN 978-1-5092-4865-0
Digital ISBN 978-1-5092-4866-7

A Massimo Domingo Mystery, Book 3
Published in the United States of America

Dedication

This book is dedicated to my husband, Steve,
to my two daughters—Marissa and Amanda,
and to my two granddaughters—Aviva and Amelia.

"I was in awe of Michelangelo's energy. I felt things that I could not express. When I saw the beauty of the Raphaels, I was moved to tears, and I could scarcely hold my pencil. For several months I remained in a state of apathy that I was unable to overcome, until I resolved to study the painters who I felt I had a chance of rivaling: and so I turned my attention to Barocci, Pietro da Cortona, Solimena, and Tiepolo."

~ Jean-Honoré Fragonard

Chapter One

Firenze, Italy

When she arrived at the office, Hadley Evans, now *Mrs. Luca Ferrari* (she had to keep reminding herself), she had no idea her life was about to change in such a dramatic way. As an art detective she'd had the opportunity to see great masterpieces up close. But there was a definite difference between appreciating a painting mounted in its gilded, vintage frame, hanging in an antiseptic, untouchable, but well-lit space in a museum, surrounded by hundreds of art afficionados carrying cameras with selfie sticks, versus breathing on and touching the same canvas that was lovingly painted by the artist centuries before.

It started out as any other ordinary day, although Hadley's days in Florence were hardly ordinary compared to her mundane life previously in Tallahassee, Florida. It began with a brief, but pleasant, walk over the Ponte Vecchio to the center of town where the Massimo Domingo Art Detective Agency was located. She greeted Gerda, Massimo Domingo's office manager, and settled herself in her new space, tastefully and generously decorated by Massimo's long-suffering wife, Francesca.

She rifled through the first few telephone messages. Again, nothing out of the ordinary. The Uffizi curator wanted to talk to her about an upcoming exhibit and offer her a job, *again*. Her gynecologist called to confirm that she wanted to reschedule an appointment she'd made to get fitted with a diaphragm. That would put off the serious confrontation with her new husband, Luca, whose sole mission in life, other than to rescue all the helpless people (especially women) in Florence who needed protecting, seemed to be getting her pregnant.

But there was one message, hastily scribbled in Gerda's undecipherable handwriting, something about a forgotten Fragonard, painted after 1771. Had this painting been commissioned by the capricious patron of the arts Madame du Barry? Yes, that Madame du Barry, official royal mistress to Louis XV, his *last* mistress, who was unceremoniously and noisily beheaded during the Reign of Terror in 1793. Perhaps this would be an outlandish claim of another large panel painting in the cycle known since the nineteenth century as *The Progress of Love*. Undoubtedly a fake. All the other panel paintings in the cycle were accounted for.

Gerda must have gotten it wrong. To Hadley's knowledge, there were only four main panels in that cycle, considered Fragonard's masterpiece, large-scale decorative works of art, originally hung in the music pavilion of du Barry's country retreat at the Château de Louveciennes, west of Paris. They were currently on display at The Frick Collection in New York City, actually at the Frick Madison, the museum's temporary home. Hadley had visited the Fragonard Room at the Frick a number of times and, most recently, at the Frick Madison, before she flew to Florence, and she was enamored of—really mesmerized by—Fragonard's *Progress of Love* series. She was by no means an expert on Fragonard. Her time in college had mostly been occupied studying Italian Renaissance painters. Admittedly, she didn't know everything she should about the artist. She'd have to get up to speed on the French painter and printmaker.

Hadley strolled over to Gerda's office with the telephone slip, still musing on what the painting could be.

"Gerda, there's no name on this note, no number."

"The note about the Fragonard?"

Hadley nodded.

"The poor Rachmanus," said Gerda, shaking her head. "I looked him up after I got the message. At one time, he received all kinds of decorative commissions from royal and private patrons. He painted small cabinet-sized paintings for French private collectors, but most of his paintings were created for the aristocracy, so his career was put on hold and his major client base wiped out by the French revolution. After the revolution, he ultimately returned to Paris to work with the new government to help administer the national museum at the Louvre. He stopped painting for the last fifteen years of his life. By then, his work had fallen out of favor and he died in relative poverty and obscurity, all but forgotten. His most famous series was rediscovered with renewed interest in the late nineteenth century. He once said, 'If necessary, I would even paint with my bottom.' He'd definitely *hit* bottom."

Hadley smothered a laugh. She had seen the portrait of Fragonard painted by his sister-in-law Marguerite Gérard and thought he had the look of a portly and jovial George Washington. It was hard to think of Fragonard, who was considered among the most important and innovative French painters of the second half of the eighteenth century, as a "poor Rachmanus." But Gerda pitied almost everyone as a "poor Rachmanus" at some stage in their lives. And Hadley certainly didn't want to imagine him painting with his bottom.

Had he really said that? And she had not known that the French Rococo Master had come to such a bad end. Fragonard's work was certainly highly valued and coveted today. "So how can I get in touch with her?"

"She wouldn't leave her name or her number. She was calling from Rome and said she'd be calling back later today."

"Are you sure she didn't ask for Massimo?"

"No, she specifically asked for you."

Hadley scratched her head. "But there are only four main canvases in that cycle."

"She was adamant about that. She claims there's another unknown painting related to the series."

Hadley's pulse raced as she recalled the playful, erotic works of the eighteenth-century artist. The four paintings at The Frick, his largest, had made such an impression on her she'd never forgotten them. The exquisite paintings captured a couple in four different moments in their love affair, from pursuit and meeting to commitment and friendship—the climax of love—and were set in lush romantic landscapes…gardens bursting with flowers and full of mythological sculptures.

Hadley tilted her head. The caller was probably a prankster. There was no fifth canvas from that series, was there? And from the little she knew of Fragonard, the prolific artist produced more than 550 paintings, several thousand drawings (although hundreds are known to be lost) and thirty-five etchings, but who, according to Gerda, nevertheless fell from favor at the end of his life. Besides, what would one of the French painter's works be doing in Italy?

All she could do was wait. But before the woman called back, Hadley was going to brush up on her Fragonard. Never mind that her calendar was full. If there was even a remote possibility that some lost Fragonard had been discovered, Hadley would shoot that to the top of her to-do list. Massimo would be proud of her if she managed to pull off that coup. Of course, he'd also be jealous, but, par for the course, he would receive all the accolades anyway. She didn't mind playing second fiddle to the maestro. She was young and comparably inexperienced and still had a lot to learn. She was indebted to Massimo for giving her a chance to work at such a prestigious agency at such a young age. An agency that, itself, had fallen out of favor, but had been revitalized by her discovery of a cache of stolen Nazi art in a Venetian villa and a Vermeer in Lake Como. She was lucky to have the job at all. She would have her opportunity to shine in the years to come.

She hurried over to Massimo's office. Generally, Gerda kept it neat when he was away, but there were telltale signs of her boss's untidy habits evident all over the room. Unfinished sweets in a crumpled bag from the *pasticceria* down the street. Hadley threw it in the trash basket. Unopened letters were scattered across his desk. Hadley swept them up into a neat pile. Gerda must be preoccupied. Probably by her new boyfriend, the doctor.

Hadley examined the art history books in the room, until she settled on an English edition of *Fragonard* by Pierre Rosenberg, a French art historian, curator and former President-Director of the Louvre, a catalogue of the artist's major paintings. Pulling it from the shelf, she wandered back to her office to find out all she could about the moody nature painter from Provence. She also pulled *Fragonard's Progress of Love at the Frick Collection* by Colin B. Bailey, a specialist of eighteenth-century French painting who had joined The Frick Collection in 2000.

She knew Fragonard's work was more than just what some people dismissed as superficial, immoral, intimate bedroom scenes, natural landscapes, gardens, green leaves, flowers, sculptures, and chubby cupids and cherubs. The Rococo style of art had originated in Paris during the reign of Louis XV. Although the market for the Rococo Master's work had fallen out of fashion during the French revolution, to which he lost his patrons when they lost their heads, and he was all but forgotten when he died, Fragonard's use of color and fluid style influenced the work of many renowned Impressionists, including Monet, Renoir, and Berthe Morisot (his grandniece). Fragonard was a favorite of Renoir for his painting of pretty women.

He was one of Hadley's favorite artists too, which is why she frequented The Frick every chance she got when visiting New York. Fragonard evoked deep feelings with his spontaneous brushstrokes and sentimental subjects.

And she had visited Parfumerie Fragonard on the French Riviera, opened in 1926 and named after the famous Grasse-born painter. She had come away with long-lasting memories of the beauty of the scenery and a fondness for the place.

Hadley hadn't thought seriously about Fragonard for a long time, but the hairs on the back of her neck stood up and her mind flooded with emotion as she flipped through the illustrations. Surprisingly, she came across some Italian drawings. What was Fragonard's Italian connection?

Hadley put the books aside and began surfing the Internet, where she discovered that, indeed, the painter had taken two trips to Italy. Born in Grasse in southern France in 1732, he and his family moved to Paris where he studied in the studios of Jean Siméon Chardin, François Boucher, and Carle Van Loo. In August 1752, he entered the Prix de Rome competition given by the French Academy and won first prize. He left Paris for Italy in October 1756 and spent five years studying landscape painting and drawing in Rome with the support of the French Academy, sketching the Roman scenery. In 1760, he toured Italy, traveling to Rome, Naples, and Venice with patron and avid collector Abbé de Saint-Non. While in Italy, he produced a series of red chalk drawings before returning to Paris. From a quote she stumbled upon by Fragonard himself, she discovered he had been inspired by Italian artists:

"I was in awe of Michelangelo's energy. I felt things that I could not express. When I saw the beauty of the Raphaels, I was moved to tears, and I could scarcely hold my pencil. For several months I remained in a state of apathy that I was unable to overcome, until I resolved to study the painters who I felt I had a chance of rivaling: and so I turned my attention to Barocci, Pietro da Cortona, Solimena, and Tiepolo."

~Jean-Honoré Fragonard

Not much documentation and critical commentary about Fragonard's art survived today. Hadley had seen his brilliant easel paintings in London and the Louvre, as well as *The See-Saw*, one of his earlier works, in Madrid at the Thyssen-Bornemisza Museum. And most recently, on a trip to Lisbon, she'd seen Fragonard's "The Island of Love" at the *Museu Calouste Gulbenkian*, an oil on canvas, a view of a fictional garden, painted in France in 1770 and first sold in public in 1784 and later in various collections in Paris.

She paused at the computer and drew a long breath. Aha. Fragonard and his wife made a second trip to Italy in 1773-1774 with one of his major patrons, which sparked the artist's fascination with landscapes and images of gardens, leading to some of his most famous masterpieces.

Hadley ran her finger across her lower lip. There was something familiar about that date...1773. She clicked on different sites until she found what she was looking for. It was by 1773 that Madame du Barry rejected the four paintings she had commissioned from Fragonard—*The Pursuit*, *The Meeting*, *The Lover Crowned*, and *Love Letters*, which were returned to the artist's studio. In their place, she installed a series commissioned from Joseph-Marie Vien. Why? No one knew for sure. It was still a topic of discussion among art historians.

Were Fragonard's canvases too old-fashioned? No longer to his patron's taste? Was the artist's French Rococo style incompatible with the neoclassical style of the house? Some accounts claimed the series was "too decent." Was the subject of the paintings too close to home, alluding to his patron's private affairs? Or were the pictures simply the wrong size? Or the wrong colors? Or was there some other dispute with the demanding patron? Were they unable to reach an agreement on price? Records show Fragonard was paid for his preliminary sketches, which must have been approved, but there was no proof he was ever compensated for his finished work. Fragonard was notorious for abandoning projects, revising estimates upward, pushing back deadlines, and alienating his clients.

Fragonard likely stored these canvases in his studio in the Louvre for the next decade and a half—either rolled up like sleeping beauties or hanging—and returned to Grasse with the four paintings in 1790. He later reassembled the canvases at his cousin's house in Grasse, the Villa Maubert. According to Bailey, "Over the course of the year [Fragonard] painted ten additional panels: two large-scale works, *Love Triumphant* and *Reverie*; four narrow "strips" depicting hollyhocks; and four overdoors of putti. Sold by the Maubert family in 1898, the works were acquired by J. P. Morgan for his London house and purchased in February 1915 by industrialist Henry Clay Frick."

Hadley knew that artists often transformed their work. Did he perhaps draw other versions of the paintings? At any rate, the Master must have been depressed after the public rejection of the work he had spent so much time on. It must have been the talk of the Paris art world.

In studying the original four paintings, Hadley noted that the artist's exuberant style reminded her of Rubens. One was of a young man offering a rose to a girl; the second a secretive meeting on a terrace where the lover scales a garden wall; the third depicting a marriage where the girl crowns her lover with roses; and the fourth a happy union of the couple reading love letters under the statue of Friendship. Cupids abounded throughout.

Only five of his paintings were dated, so checking the provenance of a missing masterpiece might prove problematic. There were many mysteries associated with Fragonard. Where were his four *History of Love* canvases, auctioned off in Boston and purchased for $1,200? They had simply vanished. And what of the series of four paintings on mythological subjects commissioned for Marie-Madeleine Guimard, the premier dancer at the Opéra and one of Fragonard's lovers, shortly before the Madame du Barry commission, to decorate her salon? Lost by modern art historians. No known sketches existed. Guimard's villa was destroyed by fire in the nineteenth century, but on December 21, 1846, four large paintings were offered for sale in Paris. Were they the same missing Fragonards? Could this phone call be about one of the missing canvases, or perhaps an incomplete canvas? Or a brand-new discovery previously unknown to the modern art world?

Fragonard made his second trip to Italy shortly after his Madame du Barry paintings were rejected, traveling as a guide for Pierre Jacques Onésyme Bergeret de Grancourt. He made drawings of the traveling party and the surrounding sites. Perhaps it was one of those, one which had somehow remained in Italy? Or one of his erotic cabinet pictures? A painting with an intimate theme? Or another of his ink-and-wash drawings? It was likely authentic, since Fragonard was so prolific, and for a long time his work wasn't well-known or even in demand, so why would anyone want to copy it? And it was often too bulky to steal.

And yes, she discovered, apparently there *were* additional panels in the Madame du Barry cycle, including *The Abandoned One*, the subject a girl as a victim of love. By then, Fragonard was certainly disillusioned with love, or anything to do with the du Barry fiasco. But he had installed those in his cousin's residence. Could the painting in question have been hidden in a closet or an attic in Italy, waiting to be discovered? Or stashed away in a salt mine, a factory basement, or at the bottom of a lake? Or could he have given it to a lover who, in turn, sold it to the highest bidder?

Maybe the painting was in a family for generations and no one realized the treasure in their midst. Perhaps it was part of an inheritance at an apartment or a villa like the forgotten Fragonard painting *A Philosopher Reading*, spotted by an auctioneer in France, that recently sold for $9 million. *How could anyone forget they owned a Fragonard?* Or maybe it was like the minor Fragonard recovered—as part of art seized from Jewish families during WWII by the Nazis (*Raubkunst*) —from the Neuschwanstein Castle in Bavaria built by Ludwig II.

Was it a portrait painting? Fragonard had done a series of quickly executed fantasy sketches, unusual portraits of people in his social circle—nobles, socialites, writers, singers, actors, fellow artists—and had either identified the subjects or they weren't likenesses of real people at all.

Was this Fragonard in pristine shape or covered with dust, dirt, and grime? The clouds would clear once she examined the piece. If authentic, it could be worth millions and represent a significant discovery in the art world. What would Massimo do? He would most likely consult with one of his gallery acquaintances who often assisted auctioneers in valuing paintings, or a contact in a company of painting experts.

Hadley glanced at the phone, willing it to ring, but, like a watched pot that never boils, apparently a watched phone never rings, either. In the meantime, she studied *Massimo Domingo's Pocket Guide to Stolen Art Theft Recovery—Volume 3*. Because of the firm's (her) recent discovery of the treasure trove of art in the Venetian villa, sales of Massimo's Pocket Guides had soared on the bestseller lists and were currently in their second and third printings. Perhaps she could learn more from some of the master's art detection philosophy.

Chapter Two

Rule Number One: Beware of the Criminal Element in the Shady Art Theft Business. Take Precautions.
~Massimo Domingo's Pocket Guide to Stolen Art Theft Recovery—Volume 3.

In the past, taking precautions translated to taking Luca along on the job, Hadley thought. But she couldn't keep imposing on her husband. He already had a very demanding full-time job. She needed to learn to stand on her own two feet and face challenges if she was going to succeed in this often dangerous business.

If the woman was calling from Rome, Hadley would have to travel to see the artwork in question. If she left on a train this afternoon, she'd probably have to stay over at least one night and she'd miss dinner at Luca's parents' house. Hmm. That would be a perfect excuse not to have to face Signora Ferrari and explain why she wasn't pregnant yet, even though they had only been married for what seemed like a moment.

Hadley glared at the telephone, willing it to ring. And this time, as if her thoughts had conjured the sound, it did. "Pronto," Hadley answered, fidgeting with a large paperclip on her desk.

"Is this the Massimo Domingo Art Detective Agency?"

"*Si.* Yes. This is Hadley Evans speaking." Hadley

Evans *Ferrari*, she corrected in her mind. Would she ever get used to her new name?

"I was told you could help me. I have a piece of art I need appraised. How fast can you make it to Rome?"

Hadley had already checked the train schedule, and the bullet train from Santa Maria Novella in Florence to Roma Termini took less than an hour and a half. It wouldn't take much longer for a cab to drop her off at an appointed place. "I can be there in a couple of hours. Where do you want to meet?"

The woman gave Hadley the name of an upscale hotel near the Borghese Gallery, the Rome Marriott Grand Flora. The painting was too big to bring to the hotel, of course. After they talked, Hadley would accompany the woman to the location of the painting.

"Wait, how will I know you?" Hadley asked before the woman hung up. The woman mumbled something about how Hadley could recognize her. Tall, auburn-colored hair, olive complexion, sunglasses.

Hadley walked over to Gerda's desk.

"Gerda, could you please reserve me a seat on the next bullet train to Rome and make an overnight reservation at the Rome Marriott Grand Flora for tonight?"

"So, the lady called back?"

"She did, and she wants me to meet her in Rome this afternoon. I'm going to go home and pack a bag." Hadley twisted a lock of her hair around her finger and shifted her weight to her other foot.

"Anything else?" Gerda asked expectantly.

"Um, could you please call Luca and tell him I had to go to Rome to see a client at the last minute?"

"You want me to tell *your* husband you're going out

of town? Isn't tonight that special dinner at his parents' house to celebrate your six-month anniversary?"

"Yes, and he won't like it if I'm not there. This whole affair is just an excuse for Luca's mother to put me on the spot and grill me about why I haven't given her a grandchild."

"Does this have anything to do with you canceling your gynecologist appointment this morning?"

Hadley exhaled. Did Gerda know everything that went on in the office? Probably, as she was the office manager. "Tonight would not be a good night for Luca and me to be together. The timing is all wrong—or rather, it's all right, if you look at it from Luca's perspective."

Gerda shook her head. "The poor Rachmanus."

"And don't tell him where I'm staying," Hadley warned.

"What aren't you telling me? Why can't you tell him yourself?"

"If I tell him, he'll just worry and wonder why I didn't ask him to go to Rome. And he'll try to track me down and protect me."

"Which he is perfectly capable of doing since he *is* a detective."

Hadley straightened her posture. "I can handle this job on my own. I don't need a bodyguard or a babysitter."

"Or a baby, apparently," Gerda quipped, raising her eyebrows. "And how do you know you won't need help? Do you even know anything about this woman? And you're just going off to meet her in Rome? What if she's a front for a criminal enterprise—drug dealers or arms dealers? What if she gives you the painting and you're followed? What if the painting was stolen? She can't sell it through normal channels if it's authentic. She might be desperate. She'll get you to verify it's a Fragonard, and then…she or her associates will have to tie up loose ends." Gerda made a swift cutting motion across her throat.

"All unlikely scenarios," Hadley dismissed, realizing that Gerda could be right. "I've gotta run. Can you print out the train tickets and my itinerary?"

Gerda threw her hands up. "My lips are sealed. But your husband can be very persuasive."

"You don't have to tell me how persuasive my husband can be. But I know your loyalty lies with me."

Gerda shot Hadley a sidelong glance, printed out the material and handed Hadley the package. Then she uttered *sotto voce* something like, "I wouldn't miss an opportunity to sleep with Luca Ferrari."

Hadley didn't want to hear all the reasons why she *shouldn't* go to Rome. There were risks, of course. But what if her success at the firm so far had been nothing but luck? Being in the right place at the right time. She knew how fortunate she had been to get the position with the agency in the first place. To have the opportunity to live and work in Florence as an art history major. Those jobs were scarce. And she was so inexperienced. She had to prove to herself she could handle a case without help from Massimo or Luca. After all, she was on the partner track at the firm now, and she had to pull her weight. With the title came responsibility.

She would do her homework and more research on the artist on the train to Rome. Hadley felt a frisson of excitement that, by the end of the day, odds were she would be up close and personal with a Fragonard!

Chapter Three

Firenze to Roma, Italy

Rule Number Two: Stay Positive. Don't Let Your
Dark Mood Color Your Thinking.
~*Massimo Domingo's Pocket Guide to Stolen Art
Theft Recovery—Volume 3.*

Up close and personal was what Hadley definitely
would not be with Luca tonight. She tried to predict his
reaction when Gerda told him she had gone to Rome for
the night, maybe longer. Luca wouldn't get mad. He was
even-tempered. But he would be very disappointed. And
he would be left having to explain her absence to his
mother. That could be problematic.

Hadley's cell phone rang. She checked the caller ID.
Not Luca. She answered the call.

"Ingrid, how are you?"

"I'm fine. Where are you? You sound like you're in
a tunnel."

"I'm on the train to Rome."

"On the trail of some missing masterpiece?"

"Something like that. Did you get into Venice?"

"Yes, I've been here for a couple of days, and guess
who has been dropping by on a regular basis?"

"Not Matteo."

"No, that nasty monster is still in prison. And the

restraining order against him is still in effect. Remember that man you introduced us to at the Uffizi exhibit? Prince Alessandro Rossi, the one with the villa on Lake Como?

"Of course."

"Well, he brought his son in for a visit, and we happened to be there. He took one look at Isabella, and it was love at first sight."

"That sounds about right. One look is all it takes with Isabella. She has to be the most beautiful girl in Italy."

"Prince Vittorio has been calling and sending flowers and 'accidentally' dropping by saying he has business in Venice, which he doesn't. I'm the chaperone trying to protect her, but Isabella likes him, I can tell. He's adorable, and he's so sweet to her. But I had to explain her background and the fact that she had been in an abusive situation and caution him to go slow in the relationship. I wouldn't be surprised if he proposes sooner rather than later."

"Well, she certainly deserves some happiness in her life."

"She does. We've gotten to be close friends, and now that I'm in Venice I've enrolled her in a self-defense course. She's a lot less shy, more confident. You would hardly recognize her, except that she's still the most stunning girl I've ever seen."

"Well, that's good news. What about your love life?"

"Well, I have to admit, it's easier to find men in Italy than it is in the U.S. But I haven't found 'the one,' if that's what you're asking. You had to get run over by a motorcycle to find Luca. I wish I were as lucky as you to find someone that great and sexy."

"Don't remind me. Why are you calling?"

"I'm going to be in Florence in the next couple of weeks and thought Isabella and I could drop by for a visit."

"I would love that. Just send me the details."

"Good luck in Rome. And tell that handsome husband of yours hello for me."

"Thanks. I will…when I see him."

"When you see him? What do you mean?"

"Well, I don't know how long I'll be in Rome, and, um…"

"Don't tell me there's trouble in paradise."

"Not trouble, but his mother is pressuring us to have a bambino."

"You just got married."

"Exactly."

"Not that I understand why you wouldn't want to make babies with Luca. I would want to make babies with Luca."

Hadley laughed. Apparently, every woman in Italy wanted to sleep with Luca Ferrari. If she didn't want to give him children, there were plenty of women who would get in line to take advantage of that opportunity.

"It's not that. It's just that Luca would do anything for his mother, and she doesn't understand that I have a career and I'm not ready to be a mother."

"Doesn't Luca understand that?"

"He's very proud of my career, but he's a family sort of guy. I think he really wants children too."

"Well, what are you going to do? You can't avoid him forever."

"I know. I had an appointment at the doctor to get

fitted for a diaphragm, but I canceled it. And I can't tell him…"

"It's not a good idea to keep secrets in a marriage."

"I know, but what can I do? Luca is so passionate. All it will take is one look from him for me to get pregnant."

"Why hasn't that already happened in the last six months?"

"Everything was fine until Luca found my birth control pills, and I felt so guilty I flushed them down the toilet in front of him. I've been making excuses about why we can't, you know, get together until I've had a chance to see my gynecologist. He's getting suspicious, and tired of my excuses."

"Well, take some time to think about it. Luca is an amazing guy. If you start keeping secrets and avoiding him, like I said, there're a lot of women out there who would love to have Luca's babies. I'm just saying."

Hadley didn't need to be reminded. "I know. Remember how jealous I was of Isabella when I met her in Venice? I was convinced Luca was cheating on me with her."

"Yes, although she was just responding to the first man who'd ever treated her with kindness. Luca only had eyes for you. Anyone could see that."

"Anyone but me. Well, the train is about to pull into Rome, so we'll have to talk more later."

Hadley broke the connection. She had a lot to think about. She needed to get her mind off Luca and back onto Fragonard.

Chapter Four

Roma, Italy

Rule Number Three: When You're Investigating Stolen Art, the Tendency to Blow Things Out of Proportion Is Classic. Don't Let This Happen to You.
~Massimo Domingo's Pocket Guide to Stolen Art Theft Recovery—Volume 3.

Hadley arrived at the Termini train station in Rome and took a ten-minute cab ride to the Rome Marriott Grand Flora. If there were time, she would have loved to make a quick visit to the Galleria Borghese, her favorite museum in the city. It was literally steps away from where she was staying. But the lady on the phone was going to meet her at the hotel, and she only had time to grab a quick lunch before the meeting. The hotel had an amazing breakfast on the rooftop terrace with panoramic views of the city, but she'd missed that. There was a small, formal restaurant off the lobby, but Hadley was looking for something casual, so she checked in and left her luggage at the front desk.

She opted to eat at a sidewalk café under an awning next to the hotel. The menu didn't offer a big selection, but she wasn't particular as long as they had pasta. She chose Spaghetti Aglio e Olio with a small salad and a cannoli for dessert. They had her favorite pasta,

Spaghetti alla Carbonara, but that was too heavy a dish for lunch. And, of course, she ordered her favorite drink, a fizzy lemon soda. Eating while people-watching was a leisurely pastime. And the historic Via Veneto, with its embassies, luxury hotels, upscale shops, and mouth-watering restaurants, offered a slower pace of life than the Centro Storico di Roma, the historic Centre City.

After lunch, Hadley walked into the lobby and took a seat to watch for the mystery caller. She didn't have long to wait. A seductive, glamorous, younger Sophia Loren lookalike walked through the revolving door and strode up to her. Why did all Italian women have to be so beautiful and curvy? Was it something in the water, or the pasta? Hadley was glad Luca wasn't with her. The woman was fashionably attired in a form-fitting gray dress and a matching crossbody bag. A *small* crossbody bag. Too small to carry a painting, especially a Fragonard. Where was the Fragonard? She could hardly wait to see it.

"Hadley Evans?"

Hadley rose from the comfortable lobby chair and shook the woman's hand. It was really Hadley Evans Ferrari, but she didn't bother to correct the woman because she had trouble remembering her own new name. She'd probably given her maiden name over the phone this morning.

"How did you know it was me?"

"I looked you up on the Internet."

"I'm on the Internet?"

"When you found those stolen paintings at the villa in Venice. That's why I called you."

Hadley smiled. She'd seen plenty of publicity about Signore Domingo recovering the stolen artwork, but she hadn't received much coverage. It must have been because of her role curating the "Lost Masterpieces" exhibit featuring those paintings at the Uffizi Gallery.

"Please, have a seat. May I ask your name?"

"Alessandra Montenegro," the woman replied, slipping her card into Hadley's hand. Hadley reviewed the card that read "Classic Italian Interiors."

"So you're an interior designer?"

"Yes, it's a family business."

Hadley's eyes fell again on Alessandra's purse.

"You're wondering where the Fragonard is and, of course, it wouldn't fit in my handbag. It's a large panel painting."

"When can I see it?" Hadley asked, trying to tamp down her excitement. She didn't want to appear too eager.

"We'll take a taxi to the estate now. Palazzo Allegretti is on the outskirts of the city. The new owners have hired me to redecorate the entire villa. It's quite a large project."

Hadley could hardly wait to see the Fragonard. But she didn't know this woman. Would she be safe getting into a taxi with a stranger without notifying anyone— Gerda, Luca, at least the front desk, regarding her whereabouts? She knew her actions were imprudent, but she chose to go with her gut. The woman seemed on the level, and Hadley was in a hurry to see the panel painting.

Hadley rose and the women walked outside and asked one of the doormen to hail a taxi. There already a taxi waiting, and as they got into the car, Alessandra gave the driver the address. Hadley looked up at the beautiful, sunny sky and inhaled sounds and smells of the city. Some people thought Rome was too crowded. But Hadley loved everything about Rome, especially the warmth of the people.

When they arrived at the Renaissance palace, Hadley blinked. The structure was impressive from the outside. Situated on a small hill and wrapped around a huge private garden with a sixteenth-century fountain, orange and cypress trees, the property was more like a castle than a villa.

Alessandra smiled. "You have the same reaction I had when I first came here. Wait until you see the interior. It's magnificent. It's decorated with frescoes and antique terra-cotta tiles. It has a library, staterooms, a ballroom, and two dining rooms, a main salon, three ensuite bedrooms, two bathrooms, and a kitchen, all opening to the central garden and onto a beautiful terrace. And that's just the master apartment. And then of course, there are the wine cellars and the swimming pool."

Hadley could hardly wait. She loved this part of her job, traveling to exciting cities and getting a peek at how the rich and famous lived, and of course, the art they owned.

Chapter Five

Rule Number Four: Rome Wasn't Built in a Day. Take the Time You Need When Assessing a Masterpiece.

~Massimo Domingo's Pocket Guide to Stolen Art Theft Recovery—Volume 3.

Alessandra showed Hadley around the interior of the 11,000-square-foot palazzo, stood in front of the Fragonard, and began her introduction.

"Twenty-eight-year-old Jeanne Bécu, Countess du Barry, the last official mistress of the French King Louis XV, ordered large-scale decorative works like these—four monumental canvases, a series representing the 'four ages of love,' or stages in a love affair between a young couple, known as the *Progress of Love.* Ultimately, she returned the canvases to the artist. During the revolution, Fragonard left Paris with his family for his hometown of Grasse, in the south of France, either taking the *Progress of Love* cycle with him or storing them in his studio. He added ten more canvases, which were eventually installed in his cousin's villa in southern France, including two additional large panels, four overdoors, and four slender panels of hollyhocks. The collection was sold in 1898 to American financier, investment banker, and philanthropist John Pierpont Morgan to decorate his house in London and in

1915, acquired by Henry Clay Frick and installed in a specially designed room in what later became the Frick Museum.

"When I got the commission to completely redesign this palazzo, I learned that Palazzo Allegretti was once owned by an Italian contessa with ties to the Vatican," Alessandra continued. "Her adopted daughter married a former SS officer whose documents were altered and his name changed after the war. He took on the Allegretti name when the family claimed him as a distant relative. Essentially, they sanitized his record. Have you ever heard of ratlines?"

"Yes, but I don't know much about them."

"Ratlines are a system of escape routes—like this palazzo, monasteries, and churches—for thousands of fascists, Nazi fugitives, and collaborators fleeing Europe after World War II. Their primary destination was usually Latin America, where antisemitic sentiment was tolerated, but also to the United States, Spain, and Switzerland, often with the help of Catholic clergy. They found sanctuary, even a warm welcome, especially in Argentina.

"The rumor was that rather than join the ratline and flee to Argentina, this high-ranking Nazi fell in love with the contessina, the contessa's daughter, and elected to stay in Italy. The authorities looked the other way. After the contessina and her husband died in a tragic auto accident, their son inherited the villa and all its contents, which he sold to a Swiss banker, my client.

"When I first saw the property, there were paintings by all the Italian and Dutch Old Masters, including some Rembrandts, some impressionist paintings, some Renoirs hanging on the walls. Here—I took pictures of them with my cell phone, thinking I would be designing around the entire collection." Alessandra showed her phone to Hadley.

Hadley's heart pounded and her pulse quickened. If the interior designer's photos were to be believed, Hadley had hit the jackpot of lost and stolen paintings—all together in one place. There were impressionists—a Camille Pissarro looted by the Nazis and still missing; a pastel painting by Degas featuring ballerinas; a Van Gogh, fate unknown, thought to possibly have been destroyed in a bombing; a medieval portrait by artist Hans Memling, who was popular in Italy. That painting, small enough to hide under a soldier's coat, was stolen in Italy in 1944 and never seen again; two paintings by Antonio del Pollaiolo, stolen from the Uffizi. *Vase of Flowers* by Jan van Huysum, stolen by German soldiers during the war from the Palatine Gallery in Florence, Italy, currently thought to be in the hands of a private collector; and a small oil on canvas by Caravaggio, not seen since 1945.

Hadley knew that many Jewish families had been forced to register and sell or surrender their art and were subsequently sent to Nazi death camps. The paintings later turned up in museums in Germany and other countries. Surviving families had filed lawsuits to get the paintings back but had been largely unsuccessful. The Nazis had confiscated paintings from castles and churches, stolen them outright from museums—ostensibly for their protection—and pirated them from private homes. In fact, between 1933 and 1945, some 600,000-plus works of art were plundered, confiscated under duress, or destroyed by the Nazis. The provenance of paintings during that time were all suspect, the history wiped out or doctored. Many Nazis sold the works they had seized, even those they considered "degenerate."

"What a collection," Hadley remarked, drawing in deep, calming breaths. "This is a treasure trove of masterworks. We need to report these to the authorities immediately. Many, if not all of them, are of questionable provenance, probably looted by the Nazis, some previously unknown. These should be returned to their original owners, if any of them survived the Holocaust. The survivors might opt to donate or sell them to a museum where the world could appreciate them, but that should be their choice. And why aren't they hanging on the walls now?"

"Because the new owner had them all removed, supposedly for appraisal. But when I called him to check on when they'd be returned to the palazzo, he denied the paintings ever existed. I think we've seen the last of them. Do you think they could be fakes?"

"The *Independent* estimates that twenty percent of art in major U.K. museums might be fake," Hadley said. "Even the world's largest museums have a shockingly high number of fake paintings in their collections. But the chances of these being forgeries is unlikely. I imagine they're going to be sold off under the table to private clients or museums or auctioned off anonymously, if they haven't been already. The paintings are too well known to be sent to a legitimate auction house in the public purview. I wonder why they left the Fragonard here?"

"They obviously thought it was a worthless panel painting, or else it was somehow overlooked as part of the room decoration, a lighthearted sexual scene," said Alessandra. "Fragonard sometimes pushed the limits of propriety. A costly mistake on their part. So now I'm left with only one painting to design around. I'm thinking of going back to the times when art had to match the décor of the room. But I'm not sure what artwork I'll be working with, except this one."

"Do you know which company was doing the appraisals?"

"They mentioned an Italian auction house—Lindenberger, I think."

"I never heard of that one. It sounds more like a German firm." Hadley gave Alessandra her cell phone number. "Can you forward those photos to me? I want to pass these on to the carabinieri to check their online database of illegally stolen cultural property. It can't be a coincidence that all these missing masterpieces were in the same place after almost eighty years. I don't believe in coincidences."

Alessandra forwarded the photos to Hadley, who sent them to Luca's friend Lorenzo in the Carabinieri Art Squad. She dared not call Luca, since she was doing her best to avoid him, at least temporarily.

"My grandfather founded our design firm. My father warned me away from this project. There were rumors that not only was the contessa's villa a safehouse and a way station for retreating Nazis but possibly also for their stolen artwork. I just couldn't resist the opportunity to see the inside of this mansion. Now I see the whole project reeks of illegitimacy."

"What exactly do you want me to do?" Hadley asked.

"I was wondering if you could authenticate the painting and trace the provenance of the Fragonard, if it is a Fragonard," said Alessandra. "It looks legitimate, but

I'm not an art expert."

Hadley searched some closets and found a tall ladder. She gingerly climbed up the steps to take the painting off its mountings. She carefully handed it down to Alessandra and climbed back down the ladder. When she examined the artist's signature on the reverse of the painting's frame, she nodded.

"I believe you're right. I would need to do some additional provenance research."

Hadley accessed the Internet. "There was an etching of the painting published in 1788. It was formerly owned by an Italian patron of Fragonard, who acquired it sometime during the artist's second trip to Italy. It was lost after it was sold at auction in 1796."

"If it belongs here legitimately, I plan to make it the focus of the room, but I don't want to spend time designing around it if it is ultimately going to be removed," Alessandra said. "I wonder how valuable it is?"

"A rediscovered Fragonard painting recently sold at auction for $9.2 million in France," Hadley said. "Hard to believe they overlooked this gem."

"So you think it's authentic?"

Hadley propped the painting up against the wall. Examining it closely, she walked around the piece, evaluating it from all angles, opening up her emotions. It certainly had all the hallmarks of a Fragonard—playful, intimate, a frivolous subject that bordered on the erotic. The etching of the painting noted it was titled *The Heartbreak*. The style was fresh, expressive, exuberant, spontaneous. She admired the artist's brilliant use of vibrant colors and the tone and texture of the energetic, lavish, bold brushwork, loose, light brushstrokes that reflected exquisite shifts in light.

At first glance, it certainly looked authentic. It was the same dimensions as *The Progress of Love*'s "The Pursuit"—318 X 216 centimeters, a genre painting executed in Rococo style, oil on canvas.

"The brush strokes are incredibly expressive, with long, fluid strokes," Hadley observed. "The subject is playful with a frothy, hazy atmosphere. The painting is frilly and fanciful and suggestive and features an overgrown garden full of mythological statuary and cascading flowers and leaves, swirls, curves and curlicues, which are indicative of his light, graceful, delicate style. The artist used his signature pastel colors—whites, golds, light pinks, blues, and greens, with a silvery lighting scheme.

"I'm willing to bet that we're looking at an original." Hadley circled the painting, growing more excited with each revolution.

"This frame is much too thick for the painting," Hadley observed, lifting the Fragonard. Carefully turning the painting over, she saw a small telltale swastika stamped in black ink on the back. "That seals the deal. One of the top ten things to do in Nazi Germany was to steal art." Hadley felt an unnatural bulge in the backing and uncovered the outer wrapping.

"It looks like there is something packed behind the painting," she whispered to Alessandra. Pulling out what looked like a diary, she handed it to the decorator.

Before they could examine it, the doorbell rang.

"Alessandra, slip this into your dress pocket," Hadley instructed, carefully rehanging the painting. As she was adjusting the panel, an envelope slipped out. Alessandra absently pocketed it along with the diary.

"I wonder who that could be?" Alessandra said, going to the front door, with Hadley stepping down from the ladder and trailing behind. "Maybe the client stopping in to check on my progress? He knew I was here getting started, but I thought he was in Switzerland."

Alessandra opened the door. The women froze, speechless, when they came face-to-face with two men who were dressed like…Nazis, complete with party uniforms and gear, including cap, blouse, breeches, badges, patches, insignia, leather belts, boots, and armbands.

If this was a joke, it was a bad one, thought Hadley.

"Fräulein Montenegro?" one of the men asked.

"Y-yess." Alessandra stepped forward.

"And who might this be?" he asked, indicating Hadley.

"N-no one. A friend. We've come by—*I've come by*—to look over the interior. I've been hired by Herr Muller to redecorate the palazzo."

"It is Herr Muller who sent us to check up on you."

"Check up?"

"He recalled that when he met you here last week, you took some pictures of some of the interior rooms and the artwork hanging on the walls. That was unfortunate."

"The artwork is no longer here, as you can see."

"We are aware of that. We need to see your cell phone."

"Do you have some form of identification?"

"I assure you we are legitimate." He extended his hand. "Your cell phone…?" he demanded.

"This is private property. I am not in the habit of…"

Suddenly, a loud slap resounded as the officer backhanded Alessandra across her face. She cried out and held her hand over her stinging, swollen cheek. The man grabbed Alessandra's purse, shook out the contents on a side table, and confiscated the phone.

So, no joke. These men were deadly serious.

"Now I will ask you a very simple but important question," the man continued. "Have you sent these photos to anyone else?"

"No!" Alessandra shouted, grimacing as she rubbed her sore jaw.

"I will ask you again. Have you shared these photos with anyone else?"

Alessandra signaled a warning to Hadley with her eyes.

The second officer grabbed Hadley's crossbody bag and seized her cell phone.

"It will be easy for me to check."

The man who had slapped Alessandra drew a pistol.

"I assume your phones are password protected. We will need both of those passwords. Meanwhile we will investigate, and you will kindly follow us down to the cellar." There was nothing kind about his demeanor.

"We're not going anywhere with you," Alessandra objected. "I don't know who you are."

"Who we are is not important. Walk in front of me with your hands up."

Hadley and Alessandra raised their hands, their bodies shaking, and Alessandra led the way down a set of stairs to the cellar.

When they reached the cellar, the second officer took out two sets of zip ties and tied the women's hands tightly behind their backs.

"Now, your passwords?" The man raised his gun and both women reluctantly complied. "You will remain here until we check out your cell phones. Someone will be stationed right outside. We will decide what to do with you later."

"You can't do this to us," Alessandra shouted. "You have no authority."

"We have absolute authority," responded the officer. "Now, if you want another slap—or worse—then please, raise your voice to me again."

"But Herr Muller…"

"Is only a figurehead, a puppet. He has no authority here."

The two men marched up the stairs and clicked the cellar door lock into place.

"Are you okay?" Hadley asked.

"I think he knocked one of my teeth loose. Who were those men?"

"What they looked like. Neo-Nazis, would be my guess."

"Do Neo-Nazis even exist?"

"Oh, yes," Hadley said. "They weren't just wearing Halloween costumes. Antisemitism is rampant across the world, especially in Europe."

"How could that be?"

"There are no limits to hate," Hadley asserted. "I've run into people like this before."

"When? Where?"

"My first time in Munich. A friend and I took a train to Munich to visit Dachau. We were checked into a hotel and asked directions to the concentration camp. The desk clerk claimed he had no idea what we were talking about. He was reluctant to answer our questions. We ordered a taxi to take us to the memorial site, and when we got close, we saw a road sign in German saying KZ, an abbreviation for *Konzentrationslager*. But the taxi driver denied that there were any concentration camps near Munich. We pointed to the directional sign and he finally took us there. It was right around the corner. In plain view.

"The second time, my friend and I took a tour of Adolf Hitler's hideaway in the Obersalzberg of the Bavarian Alps near Berchtesgaden. On the tour bus on the way up was a contingent of Neo-Nazis who were making a pilgrimage to the Berghof. It gave me the creeps when they rode up the elevator with us to Hitler's vacation home.

"The last and most recent incident was on a trip another friend and I took to Budapest. As we walked along the river, we came upon the Shoes on the Danube embankment, sixty pairs of metal shoes set in concrete along the river. The memorial commemorates the Hungarian Jewish victims of the killings committed by the Arrow Cross militiamen, the pro-German, antisemitic, national socialist party members of Hungary in 1944-45. The victims were tied together, lined up at the embankment, and shot into the Danube, execution-style.

"There was a tour guide behind us, an Italian tour guide, as a matter of fact. And he was explaining to his tour group that this exhibit was greatly exaggerated. That the whole event was blown out of proportion, Hollywood style, and was nowhere near true.

"I wanted to speak up, to say something, to deny his lies, but I said nothing. I'll always regret that. So when you ask if there are Neo-Nazis in this world, the answer is an absolute 'Yes!' "

"But what are they doing here at Palazzo

Allegretti?" Alessandra wondered.

Hadley shrugged. "With the rise of antisemitism, maybe they feel they can come out of the woodwork. The Italian government has a large fascist faction, and it's growing in popularity. In fact, the current prime minister's party descended from fascism."

"My client, Herr Muller, seemed like a nice, respectable man. A man who wouldn't get mixed up with Nazis, Neo or otherwise."

"You heard the man. Herr Muller is just a front. Someone has been hoarding those paintings since the second world war, right in this house, funneling them in from places unknown, hiding them until the market price skyrocketed or selling them to private patrons or museums for a profit, probably to fund a secret network or to fuel future war efforts.

"Who knows how many more paintings landed here and were pushed out the door? My guess is the paintings on the walls were either too large to transport or too recognizable to chance traveling through what you call the ratlines. When the owners passed away, whoever is pulling the strings was alerted and the paintings were picked up for distribution to who knows where. And who is behind this operation, I wonder?"

"I have no idea. But these zip ties are hurting my hands, and my shoulders are killing me. My mouth is bleeding where he slapped me. How long are they going to leave us here?"

"Until they realize that you transferred the photos to me and I sent them on to the carabinieri. We need to be gone before then. Does this cellar have another exit?"

"Yes, it opens out into the central garden, but I'm sure they've locked that door, and how can we get out with our hands tied?"

"I don't know, but I know one thing. We have to get out of here."

"What do you think they'll do with us?"

"They have guns. I don't think they'll hesitate to use them if they think we know too much. I mean that you and now I realize that they have millions of dollars of artwork they're about to unload. We can't unsee what we've seen. They won't hesitate to shut us up permanently. We're just two loose ends that need to be tied up, no pun intended."

Hadley shivered in the dank cellar. She'd neglected to bring a sweater, and the descending room temperature raised the level of fear gathering and coalescing in the pit of her stomach. She remembered one of Massimo Domingo's rules about the danger of getting involved with stolen artwork. She was worried that she'd never see Luca again, and she was terrified for her life.

She tried to remember the relevant rule, the original rule, from *Massimo Domingo's Pocket Guide to Stolen Art Theft Recovery*: "Don't Panic in a Crisis."

Too late. She was already panicking. And she'd obviously overlooked another one of Massimo's Rules: Watch Your Back. Stolen Art Is a Dangerous Game. Don't Underestimate Your Adversaries. There Are People Who Will Want What You Have and Do Anything to Get It."

"I wish Luca was here," Hadley lamented.

"Who's Luca?"

"My husband, and he's a member of the carabinieri."

"Will he come looking for you?"

"No, because I stupidly made sure he didn't know

where I was. And even if our office manager tells him, she has no idea where I am now. The first place they'll look is the hotel, and I won't be going back there unless we manage to escape, which doesn't look likely."

"I'm sorry I got you into this mess. I should have listened to my father's warning."

"Let's go investigate, see if we can find the exit to the garden." Hadley walked toward the back of the cellar. Alessandra followed closely on her heels. When Hadley reached the back door, she turned around and tried to twist the door handle.

"It's locked," she said, frowning. "But we're not giving up. Where are the wine bottles?"

"Are you really thinking of drinking wine at a time like this?

"No, but if we break a bottle we can find some shards of glass large and jagged enough to cut through our restraints."

"Will that work?"

"I have no idea, but I'm not going to stand around here and wait to be executed… Just a minute," Hadley said, recalling another of Massimo's Maxims: "Don't Overlook the Obvious."

"I'll bet the former owners hid documents somewhere in this house that could help us trace the stolen masterworks," Hadley said.

"I've been all over this house, and I didn't find anything like that."

"You mean you already searched the place?"

"I was just curious," Alessandra admitted. "I mean, jobs like this don't come along every day. This house has a unique history. So, yes, I opened a few drawers and cabinets."

"Did you search the cellar?"

"Well, no, that wasn't part of the redesign project."

"Let's start looking. They had no reason to suspect anyone would be down here nosing around, so they wouldn't have needed to work very hard to hide any evidence."

"How can we look with our hands tied behind our backs?"

"We're going to get ourselves out of the restraints, then look around. We're not leaving here empty-handed."

"What if those guards come back?"

"They're Nazis," Hadley reasoned. "They're used to following orders. They're obviously not the ones calling the shots. They'll have to wait until they get instructions from whoever is in charge, a higher-up. That could take hours."

Alessandra shrugged.

The cellar door clicked open. The girls turned to each other. Their time was up. No escape. No search.

"Ladies, there's been a change of plans," said one of the soldiers. "We have an appointment, and we can't be late."

"Can you tell us where we're going and who we're meeting with?" Hadley asked. Now there was no chance of rescue. If the Art Squad did get her message, they would know about the palazzo, but if she and Alessandra were taken elsewhere, no one could save them because no one would know where they were going.

The soldier responded by taking out his gun and pushing them up the stairs.

"You'll find out soon enough."

The women arrived at the top of the stairs and were

ushered out the front door to a black Mercedes with tinted windows. Hadley committed the license plate to memory, but without a phone, there was no hope of contacting anyone.

Then they were blindfolded. Not that she knew enough about Rome or its environs. A half hour later, the car stopped. When they stepped out of the car, city noises assailed Hadley's ears—car horns blaring, the sounds of sirens, trucks backfiring. Apparently, they were back in Rome. She smelled car exhaust.

The women were marched out of the Mercedes and assisted up a short flight of steps to an entryway. When they arrived inside, their blindfolds were removed.

They were ordered to sit.

Hadley blinked. They were in some kind of cavernous warehouse. The low lighting just added a macabre glow to the whole tableau.

"What a dump," Hadley whispered, until she saw them. The room was stacked, floor to ceiling, with paintings in frames.

"What is this place?" she asked.

"All will be revealed in due time," said one of the soldiers, like something out of a B movie.

"Listen, we need to use the restroom, and we haven't had anything to eat since you took us prisoner," Hadley asserted. "And we need some water."

"There's a bathroom at the end of the hall. You can go one at a time."

Hadley motioned to Alessandra. "You go first."

The soldier removed their zip ties and produced two small bottles of water and handed one to each woman. Flexing their wrists, the captives each drank several huge swallows before Alessandra headed to the little room down the hall.

"Why have you brought us here?" Hadley asked.

"You ask a lot of questions, Fräulein."

"It's Signora."

"That's of no importance to me."

Alessandra returned from the bathroom and sat down.

Hadley took her turn using the facilities.

When she returned to her seat, one of the soldiers pulled over a small table and placed two plates of food in front of them—a selection of cheeses and crackers and a bunch of grapes.

Minutes later, a distinguished-looking older man with gray hair, dressed in a tailored suit, entered the room and pulled up a chair in front of them. The soldiers retreated to the entrance of the warehouse, holstering their pistols and standing at attention.

"It's nice of you to join me," the man said, extending his hand to Hadley. "Signorina Montenegro, I'm familiar with you, but I haven't had the pleasure of meeting Signora Ferrari."

Hadley grimaced. The man acted as if he'd issued an invitation to the ball and they had graciously accepted.

"How do you know me?"

"Who in Italy doesn't know the famous and beautiful Signora Ferrari of Massimo Domingo Art Detective Agency?"

"I wasn't aware anyone knew my name. My boss is the premier art expert."

"Signora, you're too modest. Your reputation precedes you, as does the highly questionable and fading reputation of your boss. And your particular expertise will be put to very good use here, I assure you. It's a special job that requires your particular skills."

"What exactly are we doing here?" Hadley demanded, acting more courageous than she felt.

"Okay, let's dispense with the niceties, if we must. I have inherited a number of paintings, and I'm in need of your talent in authenticating and tracking the provenance of what I believe are masterworks."

"You mean stolen Nazi art."

The man straightened. "Certainly not. I have the records that maintain these paintings were legally sold to the buyers and that I now own Palazzo Allegretti and all of its contents."

"But I understood that Herr Muller had purchased the palazzo," Alessandra said.

"Herr Muller works for us. He's what you could call an anonymous third party. We've been waiting a long time to release these paintings onto the open market. I simply need your assistance in verifying their authenticity, perhaps giving us an idea of their current value, which has undoubtedly risen since they were…"

"Confiscated?" Hadley posed. "Is that the word you were looking for?"

"I'm afraid you have the wrong idea."

"If these paintings were acquired between 1933 and 1945, their authenticity is suspect. You surely aren't going to sell them at auction. They're too recognizable."

"We have private buyers lined up, and some discreet museum representatives."

"And by discreet, do you mean greedy and unethical?"

"I'll ignore that remark."

"I need to get in touch with my office or they'll come looking for me. And my husband, Luca, will never stop looking for me."

"Well, we don't want to call out the carabinieri."

So they had done their research, Hadley thought. They knew about Luca.

"I'll let you contact your office, but I'll be listening."

The man handed Hadley her cell phone. Hadley's hand shook when she dialed her office number, but she tried to appear calm.

"Gerda, it's me. Yes, everything's fine. I just need to stay in Rome a while longer. Can you get in touch with Luca and tell him I won't be home for a few days? That I should be home in time for his mother's dinner? And tell Massimo I'm really getting a lot of use out of his Rule Number Seven."

"Hadley, are you sure you're okay?"

"Perfectly. And don't forget to tell Luca that when I get back I can't wait to start on our special project."

"Special project?"

"You know, starting a family."

"You're scaring me."

"Have a nice night. See you soon."

She hoped Gerda got her message: She was in desperate trouble and she needed help.

Chapter Six

Firenze, Italy

*Rule Number Five: Eyck*spect the Worst and You Won't Be Disa*Pointillism*. Ha-Ha.
~Massimo Domingo's Pocket Guide to Stolen Art Theft Recovery—Volume 3.

Gerda listened to the dial tone with alarm. Something was wrong. Hadley was definitely not ready to have a family, and she had already told Gerda she was going to miss her mother-in-law's dinner. She pulled a first-edition copy of Massimo's *Pocket Guide to Art Theft Recovery*. She looked up Rule Number Seven: "Don't Be Afraid to Ask for Help."

Okay, that was a warning signal that Hadley needed help. Disobeying Hadley's earlier orders, Gerda called Luca.

"Ferrari here."

"Luca, it's Gerda. I think Hadley's in trouble."

Luca's voice rose an octave. "What do you mean she's in trouble?"

"Well, I don't know how exactly, but she just called and said she'd be gone for a few more days and that she was looking forward to your mother's dinner, when she knows she'll never make it back from Rome in time to attend."

"You told me that this morning."

"But some other things she said made me suspicious. She said something about Massimo's Rule Number Seven, which is Don't Be Afraid to Ask for Help."

Gerda declined to relay the message about starting a family. That was a personal message to Gerda signaling that Hadley was in trouble.

"I got a call today from my friend Lorenzo at the Art Squad in Rome. He said Hadley had texted a series of photos of the interior of a palazzo on the outskirts of Rome. Stolen art. I didn't think anything of it, because that's her business. Is that why she went to Rome?"

"She was supposed to meet an interior designer about a Fragonard."

"What's a Fragonard?"

Gerda exhaled. Of course, Luca didn't know the difference between a Fragonard and a Fra Filippo Lippi. Most people didn't. And most Italians could care less about a French artist.

"A French painting she was going to authenticate."

"In Italy?"

"Yes."

"Not stolen art?"

"That's not why she went to Rome, but stolen art is a shady business."

"I've been trying to reach her all afternoon, and she doesn't answer her phone. Do you know who she was meeting?"

"The woman didn't leave her name."

"Where was Hadley staying in Rome?"

Gerda hesitated. Hadley had left her strict instructions not to tell Luca the name of the hotel. But then she had called back in what sounded like a plea for help.

"Gerda, please, tell me where my wife is staying in Rome," Luca urged.

Gerda decided it wasn't good to lie to the police.

"The Rome Marriott Grand Flora."

"Thank you. Let me know when you hear from her again."

****

Luca dialed the number for the hotel in Rome.

"The Rome Marriott Grand Flora."

"Yes, this is Luca Ferarri. My wife—Hadley Ferrari—is staying at your hotel, and I need to get in touch with her."

"Hold and I will put you through to her room."

"I need her room number."

"Our policy doesn't—"

"I don't care about your policy. This is the carabinieri."

"Let me check with the manager."

A few minutes later, the operator transferred him to the manager.

"What can I help you with, signore?"

"My wife, Hadley Ferrari, checked into your hotel this morning. I need to find her."

"We don't get involved in personal matters between husbands and wives."

"This is not a personal matter," barked Luca. "This is official carabinieri business."

"I'm sorry to have to tell you this, but when your wife came to our hotel, she checked in but left her luggage with us at the front desk. She never went up to her room but met someone in the lobby and they took a taxi. She has not returned."

Luca swore.

"If your wife is seeing someone on the side—"

Luca was tempted to hang up the phone on this idiot.

"I need to speak to the doorman on duty at the taxi station. I will email you a scanned picture of my wife. I need to know if she got into a cab with another woman, what time, and where they went. Or give me the name of the cab company you do business with, and I'll track the information down myself."

"Let me do some checking," the manager said. "There are many people who take cabs. It's unlikely the doorman will be able to remember—"

"Then I'll need his name so I can refresh his memory. My wife is unforgettably beautiful. She's missing, and I need answers *now*! Here's my number..." He rattled off the digits. "Call me when you get the information. I'm on my way to Rome." Luca scowled and promptly disconnected the phone.

He returned home to pack, then took a cab to the train station and bought a ticket to Rome. On the train, he recalled the last conversation he'd had with Hadley. It was more like an argument. His mother was pressuring him about having children, and he passed on her thoughts to Hadley. She was less than enthusiastic about the prospect. It was their first argument since they'd been married, more like a disagreement. He knew that Hadley hated conflict. She'd humor him and say what he wanted to hear, with no intention of doing what she didn't want to do. His wife was strong-willed—one of the qualities he loved about her. He also knew she was not looking forward to the dinner with his mother. He'd wondered if she hadn't made up the story about having to appraise a painting just to avoid his mother. Maybe she ran away. Mama would not be happy that her new daughter-in-law decided not to show up tonight. And now he would have to bail on the meal Mama had worked all day preparing.

But he was worried. Lorenzo said they had been looking for those paintings in Hadley's pictures since the end of the war. What had Hadley gotten herself into? That was just like his wife. She went in search of one painting and stumbled into a stash of stolen art. She seemed to gravitate toward danger, mystery, and intrigue. Lorenzo was fairly certain where Hadley had gone. They'd had their suspicions about shady dealings at Palazzo Allegretti. But the place had been off limits since World War II. The contessa had some very highly placed friends. Her brother was a bishop at the Vatican. Her estate was impenetrable. The Art Squad had been dying to get inside and were headed there now with a search warrant. After Luca met with the doorman at the hotel, he was going to meet Lorenzo at the palazzo.

He needed answers. And he needed to lay hands on Hadley, to caress her face, to make sure she was unharmed. Everyone thought being in the carabinieri was dangerous. But in truth, Hadley's business was just as risky. He'd like nothing more than to keep her pregnant so she could stay safely home with their children. But Hadley was a modern, high-spirited, independent woman. She loved her job, and she wasn't ready to give it up. He'd known the kind of woman she was when he married her and he had no regrets. Admittedly, he could be a little heavy-handed when he was in protection mode and single-minded. He was going to find his wife, if he had to tear Rome apart. If anything had happened to Hadley, there would be hell to pay. He drummed his fingers on the tabletop in front of him, trying to remain calm. He needed answers, now. If anyone had touched a hair on his wife's head, they were going to regret it.

His cell phone rang, blasting him out of his angry funk.

"Ferrari."

"Luca, it's Lorenzo."

"What have you found?"

"We're at the palazzo. It's empty. The only painting left in the place is a Fragonard. The walls are stripped bare. But there's evidence your wife and another woman may have been here. We've checked the security footage, and two women were led away from the house into a Mercedes at gunpoint. I'm pretty sure I recognize Hadley, but we need you to verify. Come right to this address when you get here, and help us identify some of the evidence we found. We're tracing the license plate now."

"Hadley's not there?"

"We searched the entire house. The women were being held in the wine cellar, but they're gone."

Luca flexed his fingers and tightened his knuckles, patting the pistol in its holster. "Someone has her."

"That's what we think, yes. If we find her, we find the stolen paintings."

Luca could care less about the stolen paintings. He didn't know the difference between a Dali and a Degas. Of course, every Italian school child knew about Michelangelo's "David" and had been to see the renowned sculpture in the Galleria dell'Accademia. But that was the extent of his knowledge of art history. Depending on life goals, an Italian schoolchild could choose to study artistico in high school, or he or she could go on to a number of other courses of study. Luca had chosen a different direction, in the field of law enforcement. He was all about protecting people. But he wanted his wife back. If he was going to get help from the Art Squad, he'd pretend he was interested in their paintings. He forced himself to focus as he listened to Lorenzo drone on about the stolen works of art.

According to Lorenzo, they suspected the palazzo was a stop on the ratline. Men and money, paintings, and other valuables had been moved in and out of the villa at the end of World War II. SS officers slid in—and out with new papers—on their way to South America and other stops along the escape route. Stolen Nazi art was unloaded and funneled out, but in the case of the most valuable paintings, the contessa had intervened and claimed them for her own collection. They were at the palazzo all this time, building up value. After her daughter the contessina and her daughter's husband had died, their son had sold the house and its contents to some intermediary in Switzerland, a banker, who had absconded with the missing loot. No doubt buyers were already lined up in a clandestine bargain with the devil. They were going to follow the financial trail and investigate the banker and the contessina's son, untangle the mess, and see what other properties were owned under their names.

The train sped on as Lorenzo continued to talk, but all Luca could concentrate on was Hadley. Apparently, there was no need to talk to the hotel doorman. He'd rent a car and swing by to pick up Hadley's luggage. Maybe there was a clue in her overnight bag. She would not have left her luggage at the front desk and spent the night out. Something had definitely happened to his wife. His imagination was running wild. There were some evil people in the world. How many times had he warned Hadley to be careful! But she would only see the good in people. She was too trusting.

Hold on, Hadley, I'm coming for you. Luca released his hopeful wishes, like white doves, into the universe. He and Hadley hadn't known each other long, but they were somehow connected, body and soul. He hoped his earnest prayers would reach her and keep her safe.

Chapter Seven

Roma, Italy

Rule Number Six: Mind Your *Mannerisms.*
~Massimo Domingo's Pocket Guide to Stolen Art Theft Recovery—Volume 3.

"You know he's probably going to kill us," Hadley said.

"Why would you say that?" Sweat poured out of Alessandra's skin.

"To tie up loose ends. We can identify him."

"He never gave us a name."

"We know he has to be associated with the contessina and the Palazzo Allegretti, and we could pick him out of a lineup."

"But don't they need you to authenticate their paintings?"

"I'm trying to work as slowly as I can, hoping someone will rescue us. But I don't think we can count on that. If we want to get out of this alive, we have to save ourselves."

"And how do you propose we do that?"

"I have some ideas."

"How can you remain so calm. Aren't you scared?"

"Of course, but we can't afford to show fear. My guess is that these paintings are all originals, worth billions, which makes us expendable. That guy is a brute, but he doesn't know his backside from a Botticelli. He knows they're valuable but has no idea how much they're worth. We have the upper hand."

"He's a philistine," agreed Alessandra. "All he cares about is money. He has no appreciation for the beauty of the paintings."

"He's going to keep us trapped in this warehouse until I analyze every one of these paintings," said Hadley. "I'm exhausted. We haven't showered in two days, and we've hardly eaten. I'm not going to tolerate this."

"He doesn't need me. Why is he keeping me around?"

"You're his insurance. If I don't cooperate, he'll threaten to kill you."

"What a pleasant thought."

"I'm just being honest here. But I won't let anything happen to you. Stay hydrated and eat anything they bring in. We have to keep up our strength."

Hadley got back to the business at hand, and her eyes roamed the warehouse, disbelieving the treasures she was looking at.

"This is an embarrassment of riches," she said. "Do you know how many people would kill to be able to handle these masterpieces?"

"Please, don't use the word 'kill.' "

"What I mean is, in my normal life, I'd never get this close to even a few of these paintings, and here I have an entire warehouse full of them. And it might take me a lifetime to go through them all. I mean, look at these! Some of the paintings here were part of Hermann Göring's secret stash from Carinhall, his hunting lodge outside Berlin, many of them stored in his cellar. We thought they'd been destroyed when he demolished his country estate, or maybe were sunk at the bottom of a lake or buried in the woods or stored in the Friedrichshain flak tower in Berlin, or in any number of other places he might have hidden them. There was a fire at the flak tower, and we thought some of these Old Masters had burned and been lost forever or stolen by the Russians before the flak tower ignited. He had 1,350 looted paintings by Van Gogh, Rubens, Tintoretto, even Botticelli and others. These are priceless.

"Some of these paintings were scheduled to travel by rail to other locations in Germany, when Göring fled to Berchtesgaden, in Bavaria, and we thought the entire collection had been discovered by the Allies, but obviously, some were rerouted to Rome and bound for evacuation through the ratline. The conte, or his future son-in-law, the former SS officer, could have been friendly with Göring. Perhaps he trusted that rat to safekeep his treasures, and instead, the conte and contessa kept the artwork for themselves and passed it on to the contessina and her husband."

Their jailer appeared behind Hadley, who was examining one of the paintings.

"Ah, the Van Gogh. That has always been one of my mother's favorite paintings. A tree."

So he'd let it slip that the contessina was his mother. Now they'd never get out alive. But they would stay alive for as long as Hadley could prove her worth to him.

"A Wind-Beaten Tree," Hadley corrected. "Oil on canvas. Landscape art. Height: 13.7 inches. Width: 18.5 inches. Painted in August 1883 at The Hague. Stolen in 1997."

"Ah, so you know it."

"I know it was stolen from a private collection in Zurich and that it has never been recovered."

"And its worth?"

"Considerable. As you well know, all of these paintings are priceless."

"Yet we have to set a price."

"So the plundering continues. It wasn't just during the war. This painting went missing half a century later."

"Our network cannot exist without a steady influx of cash."

"What network is that?" Hadley asked.

"That is no business of yours."

"I know you're going to kill us, eventually, and I'd like to know the full story. As an art historian, I need answers."

The man smiled. "Then we understand each other. Well, let me introduce myself. I am Conte Stefano di Allegretti. My grandparents owned the villa and the paintings and works of art inside. Then my parents inherited the palazzo, and now the villa and its contents belong to me."

"Not legally. Most of these paintings were stolen from private homes and museums."

"No, they were legally purchased."

"At fire sale prices," Hadley countered.

"What do they say—'All is fair in love and war'?"

"These paintings have nothing to do with fairness or love, only heartbreak."

"The love my parents had for each other legendary. My father was going to relocate to South America. Everything was arranged for his travel on an Italian steamship to Argentina. He was an SS officer and a member of the Gestapo, charged with transporting some paintings for Hermann Göring. But when he got to the villa, he took one look at my mother and it was love at first sight. He couldn't leave her, and she wouldn't leave Rome. They married, and I was born."

"And they lived happily ever after with Göring's stolen Nazi art."

"Göring was taken prisoner in May of 1945 and was convicted of war crimes at Nuremberg, but he swallowed a cyanide tablet before he could hang in October 1946. What were they to do with the paintings? How could they possibly trace the provenance of all those works of art? Who could they give them back to?"

"They could have turned them in to the authorities."

"But then my parents and grandparents would be implicated. My mother would never have allowed that."

"Was your father a war criminal?"

"Of course not. He was just following orders."

Hadley rolled her eyes at the time-worn rationale for war criminals.

"My great-uncle was a bishop at the Vatican."

"And was he involved in the looting of artwork? Was he aware of the ratline?"

"We were protected. If some of the artwork ended up with my uncle, well, then it was a small price to pay to keep the escape pipeline going."

"Of course, there were many churchmen who intervened on behalf of persecuted Jews. But surely you know there were people in the Catholic clergy who gave assistance to Nazi officers, high-ranking party members and collaborators, even war criminals, sometimes knowingly, sometimes not. Ostensibly, they were helping Catholic war refugees. They hid them in Italian convents or helped them after they escaped American or Austrian POW camps, even furnished falsified passports. And while the Vatican remained neutral, they did not denounce the mass killings. Instead, they chose to remain silent, even though they knew what was going on, which condemned even more people to death. What is the purpose of this network you spoke of?"

"You have no idea how much it costs to finance all the German patriots who were relocated after World War II. And then we had their families to support, the future generations sympathetic to our cause."

"And I'm sure you knew that Argentine President Juan Perón helped establish the "rat lines," Alessandra said.

"He was also sympathetic to our cause," the conte admitted.

"And you probably funneled money through Swiss banks to support the network and provide fake documents, which is where Herr Muller came in," Alessandra added. "And you needed him as a front so you couldn't be implicated."

"And I suppose you had to sell off some of the artwork over the years to maintain the network," Hadley speculated.

"The buyers were more than willing."

"Private buyers?" Hadley asked.

"Art collectors. Art investors. Speculators. And museums."

"Who were willing to look the other way," Hadley offered.

The conte did not disagree.

"And what about the Jewish families whose possessions were confiscated? Who is supporting them, if they even survived?" Alessandra wondered.

"Germany has been paying reparations to Holocaust survivors since the 1950s, and they're still paying today."

Hadley shook her head. "So you think that justice was served?"

"It's none of my concern. I wasn't even born during the war."

Hadley exhaled. "But you are still profiting from the large-scale theft."

The conte shrugged. "Enough talk. Get back to work. We want to sell off the first batch of paintings as soon as possible."

Unbelievable, Hadley thought. "Do you even care about the fact that these precious works of art will never be seen and appreciated again, except by a greedy private collector?"

"These paintings are my legacy. I have every right to profit by them."

"Some wealthy patrons generously loan their works of art out for public viewing or donate their collections upon their death. What you're doing is not only illegal, it's selfish."

"That is my business. Now, where are we in this endeavor?"

"I'm making progress, but we're exhausted," Hadley explained. "We can't work under these conditions. We need to shower and rest and get some proper nourishment or I can't continue. Is there a place we can sleep?"

"Does this look like a first-class hotel?"

"Hardly. But I'm afraid I can't concentrate. And it's unnerving to have a man with a gun pointing his weapon at my back."

"He has strict instructions to make sure you don't send a message to the outside world. Because if I find that you try to contact—"

"I told you, I'm only using the computer to do research."

"All right," conceded the conte. "I'll make the arrangements."

"Thank you." Hadley made an attempt at being polite, but she could hardly control her temper.

The conte walked away and consulted with the guard.

"Do you still have that diary?" Hadley asked Alessandra.

"Yes," she answered, patting her dress pocket. "And the envelope that fell out of the back of the painting."

"We'll have a look at them when we get to wherever we're going to sleep later tonight."

Hadley picked up another painting, this one by Rubens. When it left this warehouse, it would disappear from public view forever. What a shame. It was criminal.

"Alessandra, take notes, please," Hadley instructed. "I'm going to tell you the name of the artist and the title of the painting, the genre, whether the painting was signed or unsigned, the medium, such as oil on canvas, or oil on oak panel, a description of the piece, and the dimensions. I'll also give the approximate date it was painted and my estimate of its current appraised value, and try to fill in the blanks to trace the true provenance or the history of ownership of the painting. We'll need to know where it was exhibited and any other information, notes or references, catalogue listings, et cetera, that I can access from an archive and verify records on the painting."

"How will you know how much a painting is worth?"

"That's difficult, but I can make an estimate based on what the last painting by that artist sold for. For example, the Vermeer we just processed will sell for about forty million dollars."

"Do you have everything you need to do the authentication and appraisal?"

"No, of course not. I should be doing a lot more in-depth research, but this computer will have to do. The internet is an easy way to complete my due diligence. There will be a lot of information missing. The conte has given us some of his parents' records, and a catalogue of many of the works, but the provenances were undoubtedly altered, especially between 1933 and 1945. Of course, certificates of authenticity can be forged. I can use this computer to access Interpol's ID-Art app that allows me to tap into their Stolen Works of Art Database. It has descriptions and pictures of more than fifty-two thousand items of stolen and missing objects of art. Anyone can use it—police officers, cultural offices, art dealers, journalists, art enthusiasts, the general public."

"How can you tell if the painting is a reproduction or the original?"

"I can usually tell by inspecting the materials. For example, the weight of the piece is one giveaway. If it's thin and lightweight, it is probably a reproduction. I can try to identify the age of the painting. If I hold it up to the light and view it from the back, I can check for written notations or stamps, labels from auction houses or galleries, indicating previous sales. Another indication is the material. Authentic works are usually done on canvas. Most original works will have a stretcher. I can check the signature. Luckily, the conte gave us a magnifying glass, so I can look for dots and check whether the brush strokes are real or simulated."

"Wow, that's impressive."

"I'm not an expert, by any means. My boss is. But he's not here. When we receive a painting, I always send it for verification to be chemically tested with X-ray fluorescence analysis and microscopy to test the pigment and the canvas. And we'll be missing the documents of past ownership. But under the circumstances, I'll do the best I can. What choice do we have? I would wager there's not a forgery among these paintings, just because of where and when they were stored, and with whom, and their obvious connection to the war."

"I'm sorry I got you into this, all over a Fragonard we don't even have."

"No need for an apology. I know stolen art has a dark side. If we do get out of here, let's hope the Fragonard is still hanging on the wall of the villa and the conte doesn't actually sell these before he gets caught."

"I'm dead on my feet. I hope the conte makes good on his promise to let us rest and shower and eat."

"If he doesn't, I'm not going to cooperate. Right now, he needs us alive."

"He thinks we're expendable."

"True, but he's greedy. He'll need my help if he's going to profit from these paintings. And as you pointed out, he's all about the money. His greed will cloud his judgment, and eventually, he will make a mistake."

Chapter Eight

Rule Number Seven: If You Get a Premonition About the Provenance of a Painting, Don't Brush It Off.
~Massimo Domingo's Pocket Guide to Stolen Art Theft Recovery—Volume 3.

After the women took turns showering, they towel dried their hair.

"Apparently, dilapidated warehouses don't come equipped with hair dryers or decent towels," Alessandra said.

"It isn't every day that you need hair dryers for kidnapped women," Hadley retorted. "Could these towels be any more threadbare? Talk about high thread count. These towels are *no* thread count. And that shower, with the hanging lightbulb and the mildewed shower curtain? It reminds me of *Psycho*."

"I don't know this *Psycho*."

"You're better off not knowing. I'd be surprised if there weren't cameras in that poor excuse for a bathroom, or remnants of blood on the drain."

"True. At least they picked up some decent food. Hard to screw up Italian in Italy."

"Thank the Lord. I was starving. I would have eaten anything, but this food is great. Too bad there's no wine."

"At least we have water. And the bread is great.

Better than typical prison food."

"Hadley, I know I've said it before, but I'm sorry I got you into this mess. I'm also glad you're here. I don't know what I would do if I was here alone."

"We'll be fine," Hadley said, trying to sound like she meant it.

"*Sono esausto,*" said Alessandra, eyelids drooping.

"I'm tired too, but we've got to find out what's in this art log or diary while we have some privacy. Someone in the villa kept a diary, and they hid it in the one painting that wasn't removed after the sale. These diary entries could be dangerous if they implicate the conte's parents and grandparents. I'll stay up and start reading."

"Thanks." Alessandra dropped back onto her cot, spread a thin blanket over her body, and fell into a deep sleep.

****

May 1945
Roma, Italy
History of The Heartbreak
The Allegrettis saved my life. Despite who they were and where their political loyalties lie, they took me in as a favor to my parents. The contessa and my mother had gone to school in Switzerland at a time when it wasn't inconvenient to befriend a Jew. And the conte had done business with my father's bank. When my parents were finally convinced they needed to leave Berlin, it was too late for them to get out. They couldn't obtain the proper documents. The Germans made them jump through hoops and then they changed the rules. And Jews were fair game. Eventually, my father had to quit the bank and sell all his holdings, his property, and all the

63

contents within to a high-ranking Nazi official at a huge loss. The officials promised that if they did, my parents would be free to leave. But broken promises were a way of life in the Third Reich.

I didn't want to leave my parents, but they assured me that if I went to stay with their friends in Rome, the Allegrettis, they would soon follow. Of course, that's not what happened. The contessa got notice that my parents were rounded up and shipped off to a "relocation" camp in the east soon after I arrived in Rome. At the time, we thought it was a work camp, but by the war's end, we knew the truth. My parents hadn't survived Auschwitz. In fact, they had both gone up in smoke soon after they stepped off the train. I later found out my mother had been selected to follow the women and children in one line, and when my father protested and tried to rescue her, he was summarily shot.

No, if it hadn't been for the Allegrettis, I wouldn't be alive today. They treated me like a daughter and, to all the world, presented me as their Catholic niece. In fact, when confirmation of my parent's death came, they adopted me and appointed me their heir, since they had no children of their own. I became known as their little contessina, and that's how I was addressed from that day forward.

When the contessa found me crying over the loss of my parents, she folded me into her arms and cried with me. Then she dried my tears and promised, "From now on, you're mine." I will never forget those words or her kindness or the sense of security she provided when I most needed it.

When I was first smuggled into the villa on the outskirts of Rome, at the age of eighteen, I felt like a bird in a silver cage. Choking on wealth and privilege, at a time when my parents' lives and the lives of my people were in jeopardy, I thought I'd die of loneliness and grief and guilt. I could see what was happening around me— in Germany, in Italy, and throughout Europe—to the Jews and other innocent victims. Why was I spared when so many others were hunted down and killed? And, despite hiding in plain sight in the wolf's lair, I was constantly afraid of a knock on the door and being dragged out of my bedroom by the Gestapo or the fascists and deported. I was terrified of closing my eyes each night. The Allegrettis assured me that with their connections at the Vatican—the contessa's brother was a bishop—and to the current regime—they were untouchable.

I had enough food to eat, while thousands were starving. The staples of bread and pasta were in short supply in Italy. I had a safe place, and a soft pillow on which to lay my head at the end of the day, while thousands could find no peace or comfort, but I couldn't rest. I wanted to do something to improve the situation, but I was helpless.

As the war wore on, I noticed we had other visitors at the palazzo, hidden visitors who remained in the cellars for weeks at a time before being smuggled out in the dark of night to safety while Nazi dignitaries and Italian fascists were entertained lavishly in the rooms above.

I have to believe that, at their heart, the Allegrettis were good people. They were hiding and helping Jews, right under the noses of the enemy. They were supporting the partisans. It's not something we talked about openly. They didn't want to implicate me, but I wasn't blind. I could see what was happening right before my eyes.

I remember the day Erich showed up at the palazzo. The sky was cloudless, a beautiful shade of blue that only God and an Italian Master could replicate. I was outside enjoying the warm weather when a German officer showed up leading a caravan of trucks.

"I am Marshal Erich Klein," he announced, full of swagger, standing before me, looking young and impossibly dashing in his uniform. "I am here to see Conte Allegretti." I was used to Nazi commanders and Italian officials dropping by at all hours of the day and night. The Palazzo was a way station for Nazis eager to escape war crime trials.

By then, the war was essentially over. In June 1944, Rome had fallen to American and Allied troops. In August 1944, Florence was liberated from Nazi occupation and fascist control. In April 1945, Mussolini was captured by the Italian resistance and executed by firing squad, along with his mistress. Frightened by Mussolini's fate, Hitler had taken his own life in his bunker in Berlin in May of that year. Nazi war criminals were on the run, and the Third Reich had imploded. So Nazis had shed their uniforms and fascist trappings. Their aim was to blend in with the flood of homeless refugees, with their forged identity papers, ill-gotten money, and tickets to Italian and Spanish ports, on their way to Argentina, Chile, and Brazil.

But not, apparently, Marshal Erich Klein. The puffed-up officer stood erect, perfectly tailored, well-groomed and handsome, and as confident as could be, demanding entry, keys to the castle, so to speak. This man was not running from anything. He didn't look the least bit defeated.

"Th-The conte and contessa have gone into Rome," I stammered, trying to catch my breath and hide my fear. "I'm not sure when they'll be back." I still startled at the sight of a uniform, German or Italian. My insides turned to jelly. My heartbeat was in overdrive. I was a Jew, after all, and I was sure he could see it written all over my face. Without the protection of the Allegrettis, I was easy prey. There was really nothing to be afraid of now, but I would never stop worrying.

"No matter. My men will unload the trucks, and you will ensure that they have a hot meal and proper quarters to rest."

I stood my ground. Did this arrogant man think I was at his beck and call—a housemaid ready to serve his needs for food or other pleasures?

"I am Contessina Allegretti. I can't simply let you into the house without my parents' consent."

"Excuse me, Contessina, but I assure you they are expecting me. I come on a personal errand from Hermann Göring, commander in chief of the Luftwaffe, president of the Reichstag, head of the Gestapo, and Hitler's designated successor. I am to deliver some of the contents of Carinhall, primarily his art collection, to this house for safe storage while he awaits his adjudication. The reichsmarschall has been taken prisoner by the U.S. Seventh Army in Bavaria. But I am sure it's only a formality and a matter of time before he's released."

I had remained at the palazzo throughout the war. I had never even been on a date with a man, much less entered into a relationship. So, when confronted with this German Adonis—there was really no other way to describe him—I did not know how to behave. My desire was at war with my dread.

My initial reaction to the man was fear. Fear of what he might do to me. And then surprise about my physical response to his beauty, if a man could be considered beautiful. And this man certainly was. Michelangelo could have sculpted him. Perhaps it was the sun's heat beating down that was causing sweat to pool around my breasts.

I straightened my back, tossed my head, summoned the courage to face him, and stood my ground. Fight or flight. And I was ready for a fight. "As I told you, you will have to wait until my parents return."

"I am not accustomed to waiting, Fräulein." Did he know something personal about me? That I was German, originally from Berlin? Or that I was Jewish? I decided to respond in Italian. He was such a Philistine, he probably couldn't speak the language.

"Don't you read the papers? Your kind have no standing here. You are the enemy."

The man barely hid a smile. Apparently, the fact that I thought he was on the losing side amused him.

"Does the name Hermann Göring mean anything to you?" he answered in perfect Italian.

I sighed. "Yes. Would you like me to recount your boss's war crimes? There are any number of them being reported in the newspapers. His titles mean nothing to me. The man is obsessed with dead artists, and he's not above tolerating so-called 'degenerate art,' if he can profit from it."

"That's not at issue here. These paintings need protection. In these trucks are some of the finest paintings in Europe. They must be handled with care. The field marshal has amassed an enviable collection…"

"Of stolen art—yes, I'm aware—looted from museums all over Europe, including the Uffizi Gallery and the Louvre, and confiscated from countless Jewish families and Jewish art collectors."

"Who were fairly compensated, I assure you."

"Assurances from you mean nothing to me, Herr Klein." The sun continued to beat down on my head, and I was steaming inside. My frazzled nerve endings were on fire, a volcano about to erupt.

"I have nothing to do with how these masterpieces came into Göring's possession. They were assembled by an art dealer, an adviser of the reichsmarschall. I am simply an art historian. He hired me for my expertise. I have the responsibility of protecting these precious works of art until they can be returned to the field marshal or until I receive alternate orders."

"Yes, I'm sure you're very good at following orders, Herr Klein."

The marshal's jaw tightened, and he pulled himself up to his most impressive height, which forced me to gaze up at him.

"I don't have time to waste arguing with you. These men are tired and thirsty and hungry. We've been on the road collecting these paintings from salt mines and flak towers and churches and country homes, and you will serve as the proper hostess the contessa would be. Or I'll report you."

I let out a loud belly laugh, which relieved some of my stress, although my nerves were still strained. "To whom? The Führer?"

The marshal growled. "Signorina, or Fräulein, or whoever you are, you are certainly the most stubborn, disagreeable, inhospitable woman I've ever met. Now you will listen to me." He pulled his sidearm and aimed it straight at my heart.

I know my eyes bulged, and my mouth flew open. "Are you seriously planning to shoot me?"

"If I have to. Now, get out of my way or suffer the consequences. I am on an important mission."

Suddenly the Allegrettis' car pulled up, and the conte rushed out and stood between the marshal and me.

"There's no need for violence. We are expecting Marshal Klein. Sweetheart, you may go to your room and rest. We will take care of the marshal and his men." Again the Allegrettis were protecting me, coddling me, rather than taking me into their confidence and revealing the truth about their motives. I was a member of this family now, and I should have been made aware of any business dealings, good or bad. Men! They either wanted to protect me or shoot me.

The marshal holstered his gun and glared at me. I glared right back. He looked his fill, piercing me with his gaze from the tips of my breasts, which were visible as the sweat bled through my white gauzy dress, down to my long, shapely legs. Impudent man. I turned and sashayed into the house, sure he was focusing on my backside as I slammed the door. Let him lust after something he would never have.

I was not going to be dismissed like a maiden with the vapors. I never wanted to lay eyes on that despicable man again, but I was not going to let him chase me away from my own home. My new home, but my home, nevertheless. He was the intruder. And I wanted to see Göring's paintings for myself. Not *Göring's* paintings, his *stolen* art.

I wanted to be a witness to the marshal's

underhanded dealings. While my adoptive parents offered the marshal some refreshment in the dining room, I stood, unobserved, while his men brought in crate after crate—containing some three hundred paintings, plus some china, crystal, silver, gold, and gems. When the marshal finally made an appearance in the ballroom, he supervised the uncrating, the accounting, and the hanging of the paintings, masterpiece by masterpiece, throughout the villa.

Hours passed, but I could not tear myself away from the priceless treasures. There was a delightful Chagall, an imaginative Matisse, a vibrant Renoir. I recognized a famous painting from the Louvre. And another from the Uffizi. I gasped when I saw Gustav Klimt's oil-and-gold leaf on canvas from the Galerie Belvedere in Vienna. And a Raphael portrait I recognized from a private collection of a banker friend of my father's. I drew in a breath and had to brace myself to keep from screaming or fainting when I saw the Fragonard.

It was the painting that had held pride of place in our home and in my mother's heart for as long as I could remember, in our family for a lifetime. How had it landed in this pile of plundered artwork? It was then that the truth about my parents was finally hammered home. My family was gone forever. They had forfeited the Fragonard for my life, for their lives. And still their lives were extinguished in the bad bargain.

This was my mother's pride and joy. She never would have let it go voluntarily. Unless. Unless she was under duress. The truth was obvious. She had forfeited the painting to secure her daughter's freedom, my freedom.

I crossed my arms and studied the painting.

"Are you an art lover, Fräulein?"

I jumped, so focused on the artwork I didn't see the marshal sneak up behind me, only a heartbeat away and inching closer. I wiped the tears from my face with the back of my hand and pursed my mouth for his rude interruption.

"I know for a fact, this particular painting belonged to…a f-friend of my family. There was no way they would have given it up willingly."

"The Fragonard?"

"Yes, this very one. It hung in their bedroom."

"You must be mistaken."

"I would never forget such a beautiful painting."

"Let me consult my notebook on the provenance of the painting in question."

The invader withdrew a small notebook from his pocket listing the objets d'art. There were hundreds of paintings. He could hardly keep track, but this…this one was the only one of importance to me.

"It says here the owners were fairly compensated."

"With a token payment?"

"Perhaps you'd like to hear more specifics about the provenance."

There was no need for me to hear the Nazi read the lies from his book or spin the truth into his fantasy. I, better than anyone, knew the history of *The Heartbreak*.

The Master had painted it shortly after his four paintings were rejected by the King's mistress when he had slunk off on his second trip to Italy, his tail between his legs. He worked on it feverishly day and night as if possessed. It was similar in size and color and style to the four panels in *The Progress of Love*, but far surpassed it in technique and artistry. It was imbued with the Italian style he had newly discovered on his latest trip to the country.

But the face of the woman in this painting was the face of Madame du Barry. If you looked closely, you could see it was bloated and blotched with tears. The model was heartbroken, obviously rejected by her lover. All around her, birds in the trees chirped, putti frolicked, fruit ripened on the trees, flowers blossomed, but the woman in the painting wore the countenance of desolation. How did it feel to be rejected? Fragonard must have thought. He even signed and dated it, which was uncommon for the artist. But, of course, he couldn't sell it, not with that recognizable face and his signature. Not in France, anyway. He had created it to soothe his soul and unleash his anger—no, his rage—upon his former patron.

He gifted it to his patron for his hospitality, and it remained in that family until being subsequently purchased over the years by various private collectors. Eventually, a dealer approached my father about acquiring it from the estate. He was looking for a gift for his new bride, my mother. When he brought it home, she loved it and hung it in her bedroom over the bridal bed.

On my last day in Germany, the painting was gone from the wall. When I inquired after it, my mother said she had sent it out to be cleaned. Now I knew the truth. Someone, most likely Göring, wanted that painting, and the price was the guarantee of my safe travel from Germany to Italy.

"Contessina?" the man repeated. "Are you okay?"

"I must have been daydreaming."

"About me?"

I glared at the interloper. "I'm not interested in your

fabricated provenance," I seethed. "I'm sure you confiscated it from some desperate Jewish family."

"I assure you I was not connected to any German confiscation organizations," said the marshal.

"Why are you transporting these paintings out of the country?"

"I am awaiting orders from my boss."

"Your boss will be in prison for a long time."

"Then I will wait for as long as it takes. Negotiations take time."

"And if he is hanged?"

"I do not expect that to happen. You must realize the reichsmarschall is a very important man. The Allegrettis have been kind enough to let me reside here until his case is adjudicated. The paintings will remain on their walls as personal property until I receive further orders."

I wanted to vomit at the thought of living under the same roof as this Nazi for months, maybe longer. How could the Allegrettis allow that? Did they even have a choice? But Contessa Allegretti had told me she'd placed the marshal in the best guest suite in the house, unfortunately on my floor. She just hadn't said he'd be a semi-permanent guest.

The marshal placed his notebook in his back pants pocket. I needed to get my hands on that notebook to see for myself if the provenance of the paintings, especially my mother's painting, had been doctored. These paintings should be repatriated to the families or the institutions from which they were stolen. I had some serious work to do. If I wanted to report the paintings to the authorities, I would need proof. And to get that, I would have to shift my attitude toward Mr. Art Historian/No Prior Knowledge, or at least pretend to.

According to the Italian proverb—*puoi catturare più mosche con il miele che con l'aceto*—you can catch more flies with honey than vinegar.

I summoned my inner strength and turned to face Mr. Just Following Orders. "Well, in that case, Marshal, perhaps we should get to know each other better."

Erich's eyes widened and his face lit up. "*Meraviglioso.* I would love that, Signorina." The marshal was a trickster. Since he *could* speak Italian, I would have to be very careful around this devil.

I fell into step next to him and took his arm. He didn't mind getting closer now that he had discovered I was a member of the family and not some lowly servant. His touch sent shivers down my body. He offered a self-satisfied smile. The smug bastard. He was totally aware of the effect he had on me.

"Let me show you to your room," I said sweetly.

Let the games begin.

Chapter Nine

Rule Number Eight: Whistler While You Work.
*~Massimo Domingo's Pocket Guide to Stolen Art
Theft Recovery—Volume 3.*

My adoptive parents treated Erich with respect, and
I followed their lead, even though I suspected he was
more than just an innocent, uninvolved art historian. The
drivers under Erich's command had cleared out, and he
became a fixture at the palazzo. We took all of our meals
together, and he seemed to know a lot about the paintings
he'd unloaded. He was eager to talk about them.

"If you'd like a personal tour of the collection, I'd
be happy to speak to the provenance of each piece,"
Erich offered.

"In fact, I've already seen many of your
masterpieces in museums around Europe, specifically in
Holland, France, and Italy, and in the private galleries
and homes of some prominent people."

Ignoring my barb, he took me on a tour around the
interior of the villa, talking intelligently about the artists,
their techniques, and the subjects in the paintings. I had
to admit, he was very knowledgeable.

When we approached the Fragonard, I stopped.
When he began describing the masterpiece, I cut him off
and raised my voice. "I'm familiar with the Fragonard."
I wasn't going to discuss my parents' painting with an

art thief.

"Let's move on, then," he said smoothly, walking slowly with his arm twined around my elbow.

I pretended to be interested in what he had to say. Under different circumstances, I might have been. I appreciated art very much, but I was a Jew and he was a Nazi. A toxic cocktail with explosive ingredients.

I expelled a breath. "I think we've had enough lectures for one day," I said. "I'm suddenly tired. I think I'll go up to my room."

With each passing day, much as I fought against it, we grew closer. At least I led Erich to believe that. Close enough so that I allowed him to link arms with me as we took our daily stroll around the palazzo. Our knees almost touched under the dinner table. His hands touched mine possessively whenever he was near. My plan was working.

"We're on the same floor, so let me escort you. Then I have a meeting I must get to in Rome."

"Will you be gone long?" I asked, wondering what evil deeds he was up to, what were his exploitive intentions.

"Most of the afternoon. Will you miss me?"

Like a dog misses fleas, I thought. I answered noncommittally. "Perhaps I'll see you later. At dinner."

Erich's eyes followed me wherever I went, and I did everything I could to encourage his interest. To ignite his lust and tamp down mine.

"And after?" He smiled and touched my shoulder when we came to my bedroom door. He took my hand and kissed it."

"Until then."

I couldn't wait for him to leave. When I saw his

truck pulling out of the circular driveway, I let out a breath I didn't realize I'd been holding. When my hands stopped shaking, I entered his bedroom and began searching for the notebook or any other paperwork I could gather related to the paintings. Evidence I could use against him.

That night at dinner, I brought up a question I was dying to ask.

Looking directly into his blue eyes, I inquired, "Have you ever killed anyone, Marshal Klein?"

"Contessina!" exclaimed the conte. "That is not appropriate dinner table conversation."

"Call me Erich, please," the marshal answered. "We should not be on such formal terms if I am living in your house. And no, I haven't killed anyone."

"Good to know. You seemed eager to use your weapon when you first arrived."

"I was just doing my duty."

I hoped the smirk on my face wasn't too obvious. I was tempted to say, "Just following orders, *Jawohl*?" I needed to stick to the plan and flatter, not infuriate, our obedient guest.

"Perhaps I should rephrase the question. Have you ever seen anyone being killed?"

Erich's face colored, telegraphing the brutal truth.

From that time forward, the topics of conversation at the dinner table were limited to art history, the best places to visit in Rome, and food.

"Where did you study, Erich?" the contessa wondered.

"Ludwig-Maximilians-University Munich."

"LMU is a premier academic and research institution," noted the conte. "What was your major?"

"I got a PhD in art history."

"How did you get involved with the reichsmarschall?"

"My father is family friends with Göring's art dealer. I met him after I graduated. We had long discussions about the Old Masters and art in general. He was very intrigued. Göring had a passion for collecting. His appetite for art, and really, all things, was insatiable. When he put out the call for art experts, I took advantage of the opportunity to be around masterpieces by Botticelli, Rubens, and Monet. At the end of the war, I was put in charge of protecting the reichsmarschall's personal collection."

"Ah, '*mettere un lupo a sorvegliare le pecore,*' " I said, and he smiled. I knew he understood me, but I translated anyway. "It's a saying that originated in Ancient Rome, which translates 'set a wolf to guard the sheep.' "

He chose to ignore that remark.

I couldn't help myself and threw another barb at my sparring partner. "I think a better analogy might be to compare you to a pirate hunting for treasure, or a pig on a truffle hunt in the mud."

"Contessina!" the conte admonished. "Erich is our guest."

"I did not locate the art, I merely catalogued it," Erich insisted, trying to sneak back into my good graces.

"*Scusi,*" I said with exaggerated deference, eyes fluttering without meaning a bit of it.

"The paintings are lovely, Erich. They will be safe here with us until you receive further instructions," assured the contessa.

"Hiding in plain sight," I said, unable to resist

another jab at our guest's evil motives.

"Contessina!" Again the conte.

I threw my hands up in mock defeat.

The conte noted his displeasure with pursed lips and a steely glance. I knew he was only trying to protect me. If Erich discovered I was Jewish, he could report me, although there was no authority left to report me to. But who knew what Nazi factions were still operating, what power they still held, or where they were hiding, waiting for another chance to strike. I would be wary all the rest of my life, worried that somebody would be hunting me down, looking over my shoulder, lurking around every corner. I would always be vulnerable. Never feel safe.

"I seem to have lost my appetite," I said, wiping my mouth on a napkin. "May I please be excused?"

"I hope I haven't offended the contessina," Erich said.

"No, I just need to get some air."

"Contessina, perhaps you could take our guest out to the garden with you."

I frowned at the contessa, who was always trying to throw us together. He was the last person I wanted to be alone with. The snake had already wound its way into the garden—into my house and into my heart.

"It would be my pleasure," I said in an even tone. If I didn't check myself, I was going to sabotage my efforts to restore the paintings to their rightful owners. It would be a daunting task. Perhaps it was just a pipe dream.

Erich rose from the table and offered his arm. I took it, trying not to react to the frisson of electricity I felt at his touch.

Even monsters could be attractive, I thought. I would have to watch myself around this dangerous one.

I shivered as we strolled around the garden. It must have been the cool night air. Erich pulled me closer and whispered, "I had no idea when I took this assignment I would meet such an alluring woman."

"You flatter me."

"I only speak the truth. Your natural beauty eclipses the loveliness of this garden and the brilliance of the paintings I have saved."

"You mean stolen," I retorted, unable to help myself.

"Your sweetness is overshadowed only by your sharp wit and even sharper tongue," Erich noted. "The bitter with the sweet. A tongue I would very much like to taste."

I pulled away from him and my mouth fell open at his forwardness. This was not an innocent man. This was truly a wolf in sheep's clothing.

"Do you believe in love at first sight?" he posed.

I stared at him blankly. "I've never been in love."

"You must have had many boyfriends."

"Not even one. The war put a stop to that. I've never even been kissed."

"Well, then, let me be your first, Contessina," he whispered, pulling me firmly into his arms. Without warning, he invaded my mouth and captured my tongue. I had to focus to keep from fainting. It felt...his lips on mine, his body possessing mine...simply wonderful. I exhaled when he finally let me go.

"I-I..." I could hardly fake my emotions. I could hardly think, much less talk, but my body was responding to him, clamoring for more.

He removed his jacket and placed it around my shoulders and drew me back to him, enveloping me in his warmth. "You're shivering, Contessina."

"Well, there's a chill in the air," I said, hoping he would never let me go.

"The temperature is balmy compared to Germany. Don't be afraid. I just couldn't resist. You are so lovely. Your beauty is incomparable."

He touched his lips to mine again, this time tenderly, kissing the left side of my mouth and then the right. Then he grazed my chest lightly with his fingertips. I closed the jacket tightly, protectively, around my shoulders.

It occurred to me I could use his interest to get into his room where the provenance booklet was. When I'd searched earlier, it was nowhere to be found. He'd obviously taken it with him on his trip to Rome. But I didn't want to be too forward. I decided to wait until he left the palazzo before I did a follow-up search.

"It's getting chilly. I'd like to go to my room now."

"Could I perhaps persuade you to stay a little longer?"

"Not tonight." My hesitation held a promise that there would be another night. Of course, there would be. The man would be living under this roof until the disposition of the paintings was determined. Who knew how long that would take?

He led me back into the house. The conte and contessa had already conveniently retired, so we walked up the stairs, past his guest room to my suite.

"I believe this is your stop." The contessa must have pointed out my room upon his arrival.

"Thank you for walking me home."

"I believe we got off on the wrong foot when I first arrived. I'm afraid I take my obligation very seriously."

"You were just doing your duty."

"Following orders? I wonder if you are laughing at me now, Contessina."

"No, just stating the facts. I apologize if I was rude."

"Well, the way I bulldozed my way in here making demands…"

"Like a storm trooper?"

"Now I know you are poking fun."

"Maybe, just a little." I smiled, remembering how he had branded me with his lips.

"Well, I'll leave you now." He stole a chaste goodbye kiss. A kiss I wished would go on a little longer. If I were being honest, a lot longer and a lot deeper.

"I'll see you in the morning, then."

"*Buona notte!*" I said.

"*Buona notte, amore. Dormi bene!*"

Yes, he knew Italian, all right, and he knew the game of seduction and how to communicate in the language of love. He was no innocent. *Goodnight, love. Sleep well.* No one had ever said those words to me. Or called me beautiful. Were his words sincere? I opened my door and closed it behind me. I doubted I would be getting much sleep that night.

I replayed our interactions in my mind, especially the steamy kiss in the garden that promised more. Restless, I tossed and turned under the covers.

Chapter Ten

Rule Number Nine: Breathing a Sigh of Relief When You Solve a Mystery Is Normal.
    ~Massimo Domingo's Pocket Guide to Stolen Art Theft Recovery—Volume 3.

Days turned into weeks, weeks into months, months into a year. Erich stayed with us for almost a year and a half, until October 15, 1946. During the waiting period, he never heard back directly from Göring or his emissaries, but we followed the Nuremberg trials closely and learned that his boss was convicted of war crimes, including art plundering. The night his sentence was handed down, the night before he was to be executed, Göring took the coward's way out, committing suicide by swallowing a potassium cyanide tablet someone had slipped to him in his cell.

By then, Erich had become an important part of the Allegretti household and of my life. If we needed to be driven somewhere, Erich volunteered to drive. We went into Rome to dine and see the sights. We visited art galleries, although why that was necessary, I didn't know, when the Allegrettis had the best collection of art in the world within the walls of their home. We visited beach towns on the Lazio coast, took day trips to nearby cities. Whatever needed doing, Erich made sure to oblige. He made himself indispensable and endeared himself to the Allegrettis. And, much as I tried to resist, to me.

During that time, I had taken the measure of the man and realized I had unintentionally fallen deeply in love with him—or at least in lust. Whether it was proximity or pheromones, I didn't know and didn't care. I had no one to compare him to. He was my first boyfriend. My first kiss. In the time he stayed with us, we'd gone way beyond those boundaries. I couldn't wait to be alone with him, for him to undress me, to touch me where lovers do, to make love in the afternoon, and in the moonlight when he snuck into my bedroom. He was tender and swore his devotion to me. We became inseparable and couldn't bear to be apart.

Did the conte and his wife know? Living under the same roof, it would be all but impossible for them to see how we stared at each other longingly and not gauge our feelings. And soon they would see evidence of our love growing in my belly. A good "Catholic" girl, as I was presenting myself to society, knows nothing about birth control, so I was afraid to go to the contessa.

When I told Erich, he insisted we must marry. I was relieved and excited, since I was very much in love. My adoptive parents seemed to trust and approve of Erich. When the time came for him to leave, it would break my heart. In my condition, I couldn't let that happen. That night at dinner, the Allegrettis broached the subject of Erich's leaving.

"I'm sure you've heard. They've handed down the sentence. Göring will hang tomorrow."

Erich nodded.

"Have you thought about what you will do with the artwork? The man is no longer in control of anything.

Your responsibility to him is over."

Erich shrugged, lifting his hands, palms upturned, caught in a dilemma. "I've thought of literally nothing else. I now know what we did was wrong. If I turn myself in, will I hang?" He looked miserably to me.

"You did nothing wrong," said the contessa. "As a German citizen, you did what you were told to do. You harmed no one. It's the art dealers, the soldiers, and Göring himself who committed the crimes. You delivered some paintings, yes. But if you turn in the collection, you risk your freedom."

"He can't," I protested, my eyes watering. "I won't let him go to prison or worse."

"Hush, sweetheart," he said, taking my hand under the table.

"I'm serious, Erich," I entreated. "There must be some way to do the right thing and remain under the radar."

"If he turns in the collection, he could face prosecution," said the conte. "How can he explain or justify his actions? Or ours, for that matter. We allowed you into our home and displayed the paintings, paintings that were stolen from museums and confiscated from helpless people."

My people, I thought. And Erich still doesn't know who I really am or where I came from. He also didn't know that I had "borrowed" his art catalogue while he was asleep, copied every last detail of provenance of every single painting. Before I fell in love with the man, my plan had been to go to the authorities with my proof and turn in our "house guest." My goal was to return the stolen artwork to the rightful owners, one of which was my parents. But my parents, like thousands of others, were no longer alive. How did you return paintings to dead people? To dead Jews?

The authorities would demand answers. If we knew about the paintings, why didn't we alert the authorities sooner? Why did we wait for a year and a half? We would all be liable for prosecution. We were all guilty.

Why did the Allegrettis hang the masterpieces on their walls? Then it would be revealed that they had used their considerable resources to hide and help fleeing Nazis. True, they used their house to hide Jews as well. And resistance fighters. They were a complicated couple who hid behind their titles. Whatever their true alliances, the Allegrettis had saved my life, and though their actions were at times unexplainable, I wasn't going to be responsible for seeing them prosecuted.

Should they continue hiding the paintings for a year, two years, forever? Until tempers cooled and hostilities subsided? With all the stories of brutality being reported, I doubted the furor of the second world war and the unforgettable horrors surfacing daily would ever die down.

"I know an art dealer in town who is discreet," suggested the conte. "We can begin turning over the paintings to him slowly, anonymously. We can utilize art dealers in countries where the paintings were confiscated and let them surface in their countries of origin. No one has to know where they were stored at the end of the war. The authorities will have their hands full repatriating the artwork they've already discovered. When these paintings appear, it will be a great mystery, but we must do the right thing, and we cannot profit even a penny from someone else's misery."

"Agreed," said Erich.

"We'll start with the Fragonard," said the contessa, looking at me. "I know this was your mother's favorite."

Erich turned his head. "The Fragonard is yours?"

I nodded.

"And I went on and on about it, trying to impress you with my knowledge of the provenance. Your mother will be happy to get it back."

I hung my head. "My mother is not coming back, Erich. This is my home now. I want it to hang here forever, with my adoptive family."

Erich wiped the tears from my eyes. "I'm so sorry." Then he realized the implications of the revelation. He knew nothing about me, not even my real name. I had been less than honest with him. He turned to face me. "If that painting belongs to your family, then that means you are…"

"Jewish," I challenged, lifting my chin, folding my arms and staring at him intently. "Yes."

Erich met my eyes and exhaled. "I can understand why you were afraid to tell me. Why your defenses went up the moment we met. You can't imagine that would make a difference to me, now or then. And I hope it will not change your feelings for me. I love you, Contessina, with all my heart. From now on, there will be no secrets between us."

"And we can never reveal what went on in this house," said the conte. "Not ever. The good and the unexplainable. All our lives depend on it."

"I will take the secret to my grave," Erich vowed.

****

In the coming years, missing masterpieces would turn up here and there—in an attic or in the basement of an art gallery or inexplicably hanging on a wall in a farmhouse in an Italian hillside village. Often these serendipitous discoveries would coincide with frequent vacation trips Erich and the contessina took around Europe.

With Erich's contacts in the art world, the family was able to successfully repatriate dozens of priceless works to their rightful owners or their heirs. A well-placed call to the German police resulted in a raid of numerous previously lost masterpieces hoarded since the war in the apartment of the son of a Nazi art dealer. One magazine reported the "sensational" discovery valued at one billion euros. The paintings had been hidden away from public view and stockpiled, increasing in value and sold when the need arose.

Anonymous tips to the right agencies led to other discoveries of riches. The ongoing return of artwork would either be handled personally or through anonymous but trustworthy third parties. These discoveries would kick off "custody" battles in court which took decades, but which often righted the wrongs of the past.

Chapter Eleven

Rule Number Ten: Engrave My Rules in Your Mind.
~Massimo Domingo's Pocket Guide to Stolen Art Theft Recovery—Volume 3.

"And so they managed to work behind the scenes," said Hadley, closing the diary and closing the door on the Allegretti family secret.

"There were always suspicions about what went on in Palazzo Allegretti during the war," Alessandra said. "But nothing was ever proven. Were they collaborators or patriots? After the war, the Allegrettis were generous donors to orphans, the hungry. They made major endowments to museums and schools, donated millions to Israel and to European recovery. They were well-known for their good works. So perhaps that evened the scales of justice. In the end, they did the right thing.

"Their secret was safe, until the death of the contessina and her husband in an auto accident, with some question whether it really was an accident. The family estate was put up for sale not much after the ink was dry on their death certificates. Their son didn't waste time after the reading of the will, opting to sell off the remainder of the family's artwork for his personal gain. But there was one secret even he never knew. He obviously knew nothing about his mother's diary, her heritage, or the art catalog his father had brought to Italy and his mother hid behind the Fragonard."

"That reminds me," Alessandra noted. "I never showed you the envelope that was also hidden behind the painted panel."

Hadley had almost forgotten about it.

Alessandra reached into her dress pocket and handed Hadley the envelope.

Hadley read the inscription on the outer envelope and scanned the tear-stained letter, exclaiming, "This letter is addressed to someone named Sarena Breyer. She must have been the contessina." Hadley cleared her throat and began reading it to Alessandra, *sotto voce*.

Dearest Daughter,

"If you're reading this letter, you are safely away with the contessa in Rome, which is a blessing. Had you stayed with us, God only knows what would become of you. Your father and I are being shipped out to a work camp in the East and only have an hour to pack our bags and pack up our lives. Of course, all of our possessions were confiscated by the Nazis. All the promises to your father have been broken. The papers we needed to leave Berlin never came. Your father "sold" our paintings, the entire collection, for a fraction of their value, and they have been taken away, along with everything else worth anything in the house. Some high-ranking German officer and his family will be moving into our home, once we've vacated it. At first, they left the Fragonard. Apparently, it was overlooked as frivolous and what they consider "degenerate art," when it was the most valuable piece of art we owned and, of course, my favorite. I have hidden my last letter to you behind the Fragonard in hopes that it will somehow, someday, by the grace of God, find its way to you. But alas, they have

taken that away, too, along with our hopes and everything else.

I do not know where they will take us, but at least we're together. We've heard rumors which we hope are not true about so called "resettlement" camps and what that really means. My only consolation is that you, our greatest treasure, are safe in Italy. Do whatever you have to do to survive. We love you and hope you are not mad that we sent you away, but it turns out that was the wisest course of action. We love you, my darling girl. Never forget that. Live a good life without regrets. I pray that we will be reunited after the war. But if that is not to be, know that you are our greatest pride and joy and distance cannot break the bonds of our love.

Love always,

Your Mama and Papa

Hadley wiped the tears away with the back of her hand. "She never saw her parents again. It was a miracle that the letter even got to her. And now that we know the truth, what can we do?" Hadley wondered. "We're trapped here. Most likely, we'll die right here in this warehouse. And the world will never know what happened to these paintings."

"If you're trying to cheer me up, you're not succeeding. You'd better get some rest," Alessandra advised. "You've been up most of the night. Maybe things will look brighter in the morning."

"Maybe you're right," Hadley agreed, swallowing a yawn and rubbing her eyes. "You know what I wish most?"

"What's that?"

"That I could see Luca one more time, to tell him I love him and that I can't wait to raise a family with him."

"If we ever get out of here," Alessandra lamented.
"Now who is Miss Gloom and Doom?" Hadley said.

Chapter Twelve

"What's next?" Luca demanded of Lorenzo when they met at the palazzo.

"I've got people going through records to find out if the Allegrettis own additional properties in the area."

"Meanwhile, what can I do to help?"

"You can calm down, my friend."

"I can't calm down. My wife is missing."

"You're not doing her any good this way."

"I am not going to stand around doing nothing. I need to find her."

"And we will. But it will take some time."

"She doesn't have time. She wouldn't have gone this long without calling me. She doesn't pick up when I call her. She's in trouble. I know it. I need to get to her."

"I understand."

"Do you? You aren't married. Have you ever been in love?"

"I hope to be one day. I still haven't found the right woman."

"Maybe your standards are too high. Well, when you do, you will do anything to keep her safe."

Lorenzo got a text. "Okay, we've got an address. A warehouse inside the city. This could be the place. Let's go, then. I'll drive."

"I've got the rental car. I'll follow you."

"Don't speed. I need you to get there in one piece."

Luca was in the car and pulling out of the driveway before he had a chance to reply.

Chapter Thirteen

"How are we coming?" Allegretti asked, pacing the concrete floor in front of Hadley. "Any appraisals ready?"

"I've just finished assessing the Renoir," Hadley reported. "I think you'll be pleased with the numbers."

"Good. I have an interested client standing by. What can we get for it?"

While Hadley and Allegretti were distracted with financial details about the Renoir, Alessandra wandered among the paintings, hoping to find a cell phone or a landline or even a weapon, something that could help them escape. No such luck.

"There's something I've been wondering about," Hadley asked the conte. "Of all the paintings, why did you leave the Fragonard hanging at the palazzo? Did you overlook it? You have to know how valuable it is."

The conte paused. "Of course I know its worth. It was my mother's favorite. But there was a strict provision in her will that the painting never be removed from the palazzo."

Hayley nodded. She guessed there was still some honor among thieves.

"My parents were soft-hearted, what you would call 'do-gooders,' " sneered the count. "They gave away many works in their priceless art collection, the inheritance I was entitled to. They loved each other passionately, but there was no room in their lives for me. They would go on frequent trips and come back with empty suitcases. They weren't fooling anyone. The paintings on our walls were disappearing at a rapid rate. I put a stop to that."

Hadley wondered if there was more to that implication than stated. Did he have anything to do with his parents' "accidental" deaths? That was a likely scenario. But it would hardly help their situation if she pursued that line of questioning.

When Allegretti walked off to make a phone call and seal the deal with his illicit private buyer, Hadley whispered to Alessandra, "I think I can hold him off by slowing the pace of the appraisals. There are enough paintings here to keep us occupied for months. He already has private buyers lined up. We have to stop him from selling these paintings or the world will never see them again. They'll be hoarded away by some rich gangster or oil tycoon or media magnate or Arab prince or Russian oligarch."

"Somebody's got to notice we're missing before then."

"I'm sure my husband has already alerted the authorities. If I'm out of communication for more than a few hours, he gets worried. He's very protective and relentless. Like a tiger or a fearless bloodhound. He won't stop until he tracks me down. And I'm sure my office has begun to get suspicious. We've been out of touch longer than expected. I told our office manager not to tell Luca where I was, but then on the last call to her I hope she got the message that I'm in trouble. And she would have a hard time lying to Luca. Everybody does. He has a way of charming information out of people."

"How does he do that?"

"All it takes is one look. He's irresistible. When I look at him, I swoon, and so does every other woman in the vicinity."

"So he's conceited?"

"Not at all. If you see him, you'd understand. I even forgave him after he arrested me."

"He arrested you?"

"Well, he gave me a ticket for walking in the street. That's how we met."

"But everyone walks in the street in Florence."

"Exactly."

"If he's so magnificent, why did you want to hide from him in the first place?"

"It's a long story."

"I have nowhere else to be."

"He has mother issues. We just got married and he, or rather his mother, is anxious for us to have children. And I'm not ready. I don't want to give up my career."

"Don't you want to have children?"

"Yes, but not so soon."

"Why can't you have both, children and a career?"

"My job keeps me very busy. I travel a lot."

"I'm sure your mother-in-law would be happy to watch the baby."

"Yes, she would. And now it may be too late."

"What do you mean?"

"What if we never get out of here? What if Luca can't find me and I never see him again? I would give anything to have more time with him. And I wish now we could start that family he dreams of. He will make a wonderful father."

"How do you know?"

"Because he is very devoted to Bocelli."

"Andrea Bocelli, the tenor?"

"No, his dog, Bocelli. And when Luca's away, he stops singing. He gets depressed."

"His dog sings?"

"Yes, he really does, like Andrea Bocelli. When Luca sings in the shower, Bocelli accompanies him."

"Well, then we have to try to figure out a way to get out of here. I have to get a look at this singing dog. And now I can't get that image of Luca in the shower out of my head. You need to get back to your hunky husband, and I want to get a look at him, too."

"Agreed. What about you? Do you have someone special in your life?"

"Not yet. I have high standards."

"Standards tend to go out the window when you fall in love. For Luca and me, it was entirely unexpected. I wasn't looking for love but it found me."

Chapter Fourteen

"I'm going in," Luca said, pulling out his gun.

"Luca, you can't just bust down the door. We don't have a search warrant."

"The car is here, the same car that was at the villa and that drove away with my wife. You have proof that Allegretti owns the warehouse."

"But that's not enough to break into a building and search the premises."

"Do you doubt the artwork is here?"

"No. I have a strong suspicion we will find what we're looking for in this building."

"Then we need to go in. Hadley could be in trouble."

"We'll sit on the building and watch it until the search warrant comes through."

"I'm not going to sit on my hands and wait for permission when my wife's life is at stake."

"We have no evidence of that. We have to follow the law. Millions of dollars in artwork are on the line."

"I don't care about your damn artwork. I care about my wife and I'm going in."

"Luca, I promise you. We will sit here, and if she comes out we'll get her, but we have no idea what we'll be walking into. We need to wait for the warrant and for backup."

"I don't have the patience to wait."

"Hold on, Luca, there's a truck pulling up. It's some

kind of food delivery."

"I'm going to talk to the delivery guy," Luca said, striding over.

"It would be better if you waited—Luca, come back here." Lorenzo shook his head, knowing it was useless to stop a man in love.

Luca strode fearlessly over to the delivery vehicle and confronted the driver. He was young, in his late teens.

"Excuse me, may I ask what you're delivering to this warehouse?"

The boy looked up at Luca. "An order from the restaurant."

"For how many people?"

"Five."

"I'll give you fifty euros if you let me deliver the order."

"Sure," said the boy, handing over the bags and boxes of delicious-smelling food.

Luca walked to the entrance of the warehouse. He looked through the orders. If he could guess which one was Hadley's, he could slip in a note. But he doubted the kidnapper would give his hostage a choice of entrees. If there was an order of Spaghetti alla Carbonara, Hadley's favorite, he might risk it. But if there was a chance the kidnapper would read the note, then it wasn't worth risking Hadley's life.

An armed man dressed in a Nazi uniform opened the door when Luca knocked firmly. Luca stared at him in disbelief. What was going on?

"Delivery from Giuseppe's," Luca announced.

"I'll take that," said the guard. Luca handed over the order and took the opportunity to peer inside the low-lit building. It was almost nightfall and not easy to discern, but he made out hundreds of paintings propped up against the walls. He edged in closer while the guard was hunting for change for a tip. That's when he saw her. Hadley!

Turn around, cara mia, Luca urged silently, his heart beating madly. *See me. I'm right here!* It took all his control not to run to her.

Hadley was facing away from him, in deep conversation with another woman.

"Dinner's here," said an older man, most likely the Conte Allegretti.

"Here's your tip," said the guard.

"Thank you," Luca managed, his hands shaking as he grasped and pocketed the money. She was right here. He could see her, almost touch her. His first instinct was to rush to her side, to rescue her. But if he acted alone, he could put her in danger, and that was the last thing he wanted to do. He took one last longing look and turned away. Assessing the situation, he now knew what they were up against. He counted Hadley, the other woman, the Conte Allegretti, and two guards.

He rushed back to Lorenzo. "Call Giuseppe's and see who ordered the food. That's your proof. She's here. She's right inside. I saw her. I wanted to go in, but—"

"You did the right thing. I'm glad you kept your head about you. I'm expecting the search warrant to come in any minute. Backup is on the way. We're going to do this by the book."

Luca paced up and down the length of the car. "There's artwork propped up against the walls all over the warehouse. I wonder how far they'd go to protect it."

"If that's the stash I think it is, there's no limit to

what they'd do."

"Even murder?"

"If they have to. They've already kidnapped two women. They'll want to tie up loose ends."

"Why haven't you tried to prosecute him before?" Luca wondered.

"We've had our eye on the count and his collection for some time, but his family is connected. If we can catch them with the stolen artwork, we have a chance to prosecute. Many of those paintings were not reported missing because their owners were victims of the Holocaust and there was no one left to speak for them. People who visited the villa were told many of the paintings were reproductions of the originals. It's very complicated."

To Luca, the situation was simple. There were no gray areas. He was going in, and nothing was going to stop him. "They delivered food for five people. Hadley and the decorator, the Conte Allegretti, and I saw two guards dressed in Nazi uniforms. We could take them by surprise, just the two of us."

"I don't want to risk it, Luca. I promise, we will get your wife out."

"You can't guarantee it."

"I assure you, we've got this, Luca."

Luca was anything but assured. He was already second-guessing himself. He should have barged in and rescued his wife when he had the chance. If anything happened to Hadley, he would never forgive himself.

Chapter Fifteen

Hadley shivered as the wind barreled through the opening of the wooden warehouse. She looked at the door as it slammed shut and thought she saw—no, felt, smelled—something, someone, a familiar scent. A comforting presence.

No, it couldn't be. She was losing it. Luca was definitely not here. If he had been, he would have charged in and rescued her immediately. Maybe he hadn't seen her. Or maybe her mind was playing tricks. She so wanted it to be Luca.

She shook her head to clear the cobwebs. She was overtired and overwrought. She had to focus instead of hoping for some fantasy ending.

"Are you okay?" Alessandra wondered.

"Yes, I'm fine. I just thought for a minute that—well, it's nothing."

"Dinner's here," the count said.

"I'm starving," said Hadley.

Hadley and Alessandra ate quietly. Hadley's hopes soared. *Luca, were you here? My darling, can you hear my heart calling out to you? Do you even know where I am? Please, hurry. Find me, my love.*

"Do you think the count is really dangerous?" Alessandra asked. "I mean, he's royalty. Would he actually hurt us?"

"Have you heard of Count Dracula? He had us

kidnapped. Of course he'd hurt us. And he can't afford to let us live. We know too much."

Chapter Sixteen

"We've got the green light," announced Lorenzo, checking his text messages. Several carabinieri cars pulled up to the warehouse, lights extinguished and sirens silenced. "Backup has arrived. I'll brief my people on the operation. They'll go in the back entrance and we'll go in the front. You focus on getting Hadley and the interior designer out. We'll worry about the guards and the count. Are you ready to go in?"

"I've been ready." Luca fingered his weapon and paced the parking lot as he cautioned himself to, "*Stai calmo.*" But how could he keep calm when his wife was in danger? If he didn't get his hands on Hadley soon, he was going to combust. If anyone had hurt her, he would make them pay.

When he and Lorenzo got to the front door, Luca rang the bell. The same guard he'd encountered before came to the door.

"Delivery from Giuseppe's."

"*Che succede?*"

"I'll tell you the story," Luca yelled, grabbing the soldier by the collar with his left hand and slamming his right fist into the man's face, dearly hoping he'd broken something. The man collapsed in a heap on the warehouse floor. Luca grabbed the man's weapon and pulled his own gun. While Lorenzo hurried in, shouts of "Carabinieri" and sounds of a scuffle could be heard toward the back of the room.

An elderly gentleman dressed in a suit entered the room. "*Chi sei*?"

"We're the carabinieri," Lorenzo announced, spinning the man around and securing his hands in flexi-cuffs.

"This is private property," the man objected. "You have no right to be here."

Lorenzo pulled out his search warrant, proceeded to read the man his rights, and called out multiple counts of kidnapping and art theft.

"Where are they?" Luca demanded, getting up in the man's face.

"Luca?" Hadley shouted from the back of the room. She and another woman had hidden behind a large painting, until she heard his voice.

"Hadley, *cara*, I'm here."

Hadley ran into Luca's embrace. "You found me!"

Luca pocketed his Beretta 92FS pistol and lifted Hadley off the floor, twirling her around in his arms. He never wanted to let her go.

"I thought… I was worried that… When I couldn't find you, I…"

"I'm okay. I'm okay. I'm so happy to see you!"

When he placed Hadley on the ground, Alessandra took her aside and whispered, "How could you not want to make babies with *him*?"

"I guess it's true what they say. You don't appreciate what you have until you lose it or think you're going to lose it. I assure you I'm going to make up for lost time."

Alessandra went over to Lorenzo. "Thank you. I thought we'd never get out of this awful place."

Lorenzo looked into Alessandra's eyes and couldn't stop staring. She looked right back. Then he turned his gaze away and looked around the room in amazement, taking in the masterpieces. "I don't believe what I'm seeing."

"This was part of Hermann Göring's private stash," Hadley explained. "These masterpieces have been missing since the end of the war."

"But I don't understand," Lorenzo said. "How is this possible?"

Hadley handed Lorenzo the diary and a catalogue of paintings she'd received from the count. "It's all in here. The story and the provenances of each of the stolen paintings. You got here just in time. In a matter of days, these paintings would be on their way out the door into the underworld, sold to private dealers, brokers, and art hoarders."

"But the war has been over for almost eighty years. Why did he wait so long to sell them?"

"From what I could gather, his mother wouldn't allow them to be sold off until her husband died, so he would be protected. But there's a lot more to the story. His parents repatriated as many paintings as they could. However, as soon as his parents were killed in that car accident, the count was on a mission to get rid of the remaining artwork and sell it for a profit. All but a priceless Fragonard that's still hanging on the wall of the palazzo. The contessina had a provision in her will that it should never leave the premises. It was the key to solving the mystery."

"He waited a long time."

"Just like the former Prince Charles. He waited almost his whole life to become King of England."

Lorenzo shook his head and ordered, "Lock this place up. And station guards inside and around the building. We'll be back tomorrow morning to start the inventory."

"I'd like to be involved," Hadley requested.

"Of course. We'll need your expertise."

"Right now, I need my wife," Luca interrupted, squeezing the breath out of Hadley. "She is going to take a few well-deserved days off."

"Understood," said Lorenzo. "We can go. Luca, you have your car." He turned to Alessandra and noted she was not wearing a wedding ring. "Signorina, may I drop you somewhere?"

Alessandra blushed. "My apartment is not far from here. Could you take me there?"

"Certainly. And I'll pick you up for breakfast before we start to make sense of this miraculous find. If you don't mind helping with the investigation by answering a few questions, that is."

Alessandra looked at the handsome carabinieri, whom she wanted to get to know better. And from the way he was looking at her, he had the same idea in mind.

"I will make myself available to you," she said, meaning it in every sense of the word. "And I'd love to have breakfast."

Alessandra smiled at Hayley, indicating that she might have met Mr. Right. And intimating that they might not be waiting until breakfast before they saw each other again.

Chapter Seventeen

Luca and Hadley were in her room at the Rome Marriott Grand Flora at last.

Luca had not said anything during the drive to the hotel, knowing there would be plenty of time for questions later. Now, in the room she had reserved, he couldn't stop looking at his wife, reaching out an arm to touch her, making sure she was really okay. That he wasn't imagining her.

Luca couldn't wait to be with Hadley. But she held out her hand.

"Luca, there's something I have to tell you," Hadley said, softly, as Luca started to undress her. "Need to tell you."

"We can talk later. I want to go to bed."

"No, I need to tell you now before I lose my nerve," Hadley replied. "I haven't been honest with you about wanting to start a family." Honesty could destroy a relationship, she knew.

Luca frowned and faced his wife. "I thought you wanted to have children."

"I do, but not this fast. I didn't think I was ready. I have so much to learn about the art detective business. I love my job, and I want to have a career."

"I understand. You are so good at what you do, and why shouldn't you work if you want to. I think you can teach your boss a lot. I think you are keeping the lights on at that place."

"But how can I keep working and raise a family?" Hadley hesitated. "I made an appointment to see a doctor before I came to Rome, but I rescheduled."

"A doctor? Are you sick?"

"No. I was looking into ways *not* to get pregnant."

"*Not* to get pregnant? I don't understand."

"I was avoiding you because I didn't know how to tell you, and when we're together, well, I know what always happens when we're together."

Luca frowned. "I thought we were on the right page."

Hadley tilted her head and pursed her lips. "Oh, you mean on the *same* page."

"Yes, what I said."

"We are," said Hadley, smiling. "It just took me a little longer to come around. I mean I can imagine a little Luca running around the house."

"Or a little Hadley," Luca said.

"I just thought we could wait a while longer. I mean, we just got married."

"Hadley, I will do anything for you. If you want to wait to start our family, I understand. My mother, she is a different color horse."

"You mean a horse of a different color."

"Yes, but *cara*, I don't want you to hide anything from me anymore," Luca said, holding Hadley's hands in his and staring into her eyes. "Promise me."

Hadley squeezed Luca's hands. "I promise. But when we were apart, I realized just how much you mean to me. I was afraid I would never see you again. And I decided I don't want to wait anymore. I want to start a family as soon as possible."

"If my mother wants us to have a baby, I'm sure she would love to watch our child while you work. If you are ready, I am ready. How soon did you have in mind?"

Hadley reached up to kiss Luca's lips. "Now is a good time."

"I was hoping you'd say that. But you are exhausted. You've been through a lot."

"I am tired, but I want to go to bed with you."

"I was hoping you'd say that."

Hadley sighed. She could hardly wait to get started delving more deeply into the mysterious missing masterpieces, on her next day back at work. She would put in some hours with Lorenzo at the warehouse, answer his questions, but then the real work would start after the artwork was transferred to Florence. She had a lot to discuss with Massimo to get her boss up to speed. He would be ecstatic and remain front and center all over this story once it hit the news—the biggest cache of stolen art since the war, and right in their backyard.

But she was going to take a few days off to relax and relieve the stress of the past week. Tonight, her focus would be on the man in front of her—her handsome, considerate, courageous, amazing husband. There were other ways to relieve stress, after all.

Whatever obstacles lay ahead, she knew she and Luca would overcome them, together. She was ready to get on with her life. If that included a baby or babies, then she would happily welcome them into the family and fit her work schedule around them. Luca's mother would ultimately forgive her for missing the special dinner, if she knew there was a possibility of grandchildren on the way. Because she loved her son, she would want to see him happy. And Hadley was going to make her husband very happy.

Hadley loved Luca, and she reached up to kiss his eager lips, anxious to show him just how much.

Epilogue

Firenze, Italy

Hadley got dressed after her exam and sat in the doctor's office, waiting for her gynecologist. While she waited, she thought about all the events of the past few weeks and the talk she'd had with her boss. To say Massimo was elated about the find in Rome was an understatement.

"Hadley, you've done it again," Massimo had exclaimed. "You've accomplished the impossible. You went to Rome to appraise a single Fragonard and came back with the biggest art find since the war, maybe ever. You've put us back on the map."

As much as Massimo waxed on about Hadley's role in the discovery, she knew her boss would take the lion's share of credit. He was the face of the firm, after all. He was already primping for his next television interview, posing with the missing masterpieces, which had been transferred to Florence so Hadley and Massimo could continue their work. But Hadley knew she had been instrumental in helping the Carabinieri Art Squad close in on a major art theft ring that had been operating under the radar for almost eighty years. There were newspaper articles and TV news stories about the ratline and the role the stolen art and plunder had played in keeping the Nazis in South America and throughout the world operating and the perpetrators in comfort.

It wasn't just a fluke. She had made a real difference in helping the Massimo Domingo Art Detective Agency attain its former level of prestige. Massimo was fielding calls from newspaper and magazine reporters and broadcasters all over Europe and the United States about *his* pivotal role in the case. The office phones were ringing like church bells. New cases were pouring into the firm on a regular basis. They were going to have to hire additional staff. On the other end of the line were new clients, excited about the discovery and anxious to employ the agency in search of their missing artwork. And, more often than not, when people called, they asked for her, not Massimo. To be fair, Massimo had given her another hefty raise and a generous bonus and was making noises about a partnership.

Word from the Art Squad had gotten around. People in the know knew Hadley was responsible for the firm's newfound success, and she had been fielding job offers from museums around the world. She had considered each one, but for now, she had no reason to leave Florence. Luca was here. He would never leave Florence, his job, or his mama. And here was also where she wanted to be. She wasn't in the business for the accolades or the money. She truly loved her work, and she would do it for free. And she felt guilty about the thought of deserting Massimo when he needed her most. He had hired her just out of college and had taken a chance on her when no one else would. He appreciated her loyalty.

Her cell phone rang, and she answered it. She'd meant to turn off the ringer in the doctor's office, but she had so many things on her mind she'd forgotten. It was her friend Ingrid Adelman.

"Hi, Ingrid, are you in town?"

"Yes, Isabella and I have checked into the hotel, and we can't wait to see you and Luca for dinner tonight. And I've got some news. Prince Vittorio is also here. He asked Isabella to marry him last night, and she said yes. You should see the ring! It's a family heirloom, and it's gorgeous. Isabella is walking around on a cloud. I've never seen her so happy. My days of chaperoning the couple are over. He won't leave her side."

Hadley screeched. "That is wonderful news. I can't wait to see you both, and Prince Charming and the ring. Oh, I've got to go. The doctor's here."

"Hadley, the doctor? Are you okay?"

"I'm fine. I'm sure it's nothing. I'll talk to you tonight." Hadley hung up the phone.

"Dr. Abbatelli," Hadley said, twisting her fingers in her lap. Doctors in general made her nervous. Her blood pressure had risen when the nurse took it. Blame it on white coat syndrome. She didn't think anything was wrong, but usually the doctor dismissed her from the examination room, while this time she had requested Hadley talk privately in her office. Her life was coming together. She had everything she wanted. Why did the doctor need to talk to her?

Dr. Abbatelli settled into her chair. "I noticed that your original appointment was to be fitted for a diaphragm, and then you canceled."

"Yes, I changed my mind," said Hadley. "I just wanted to be checked out to make sure that when I was ready to start a family, everything was okay. I mean, I'm not looking to get pregnant right away, but I'm not going to do anything to prevent a pregnancy. If it happens, it

116

happens, so I figured I'd just let nature take its course."
Hadley knew she was running on and she should just stop
blabbering and listen to what the doctor had to say.
Maybe she had found something irregular during the
checkup. Or why else would she need to see Hadley
privately in her office?

Dr. Abbetelli smiled. "Well, Hadley, apparently,
nature has already taken its course. You're pregnant."

Hadley inhaled. Well, how could that have
happened so fast? Was it even possible? "But how—?"
was all she could manage.

"The fact that you're pregnant leads me to believe
that you know how," Dr. Abbatelli said with a laugh.
"It's still early, but how do you feel about this
development?"

Hadley's hand flew to her heart. Feel? How did she
feel? Honestly, a little unprepared. Partially, in shock.
Overwhelmed. But now that it was a reality, she
felt...gloriously happy. She knew exactly when this
baby had been conceived. At the hotel in Rome after
Luca had rescued her. And she knew, without a doubt,
that Luca was going to be thrilled, and his mother would
be over the moon. And that he was going to be the best
father ever. That they were in this together and that
everything would be all right. She would keep working,
but there would be enough room in her heart for the new
addition to their family.

"I feel excited, Dr. Abbatelli," Hadley answered
honestly. "Thank you."

"Don't thank me," she said, smiling. "I had nothing
to do with it. Make sure to see my nurse about setting up
some visits and grab some pamphlets on the way out.
Congratulations."

There would be a lot to celebrate tonight.

****

The group gathered at Antonio's, Hadley's favorite restaurant, and she hugged Gina, the owner, and went back into the kitchen to greet Antonio, the chef and Gina's husband.

"How's my chef?" Antonio asked. Antonio had been referring to her as his chef ever since he had taught her the basics of boiling water and cooking Italian in time to impress her mother-in-law at Hadley and Luca's wedding dinner.

"*Ho fame!*" she said, whispering, "I'm eating for two."

"*Auguri!*" Antonio exclaimed. "Does Luca know?"

"I just found out this afternoon, and he's coming here directly from work. I'm going to announce it tonight, and we're also celebrating the engagement of my friend Isabella, who has just come in from Venice. There will be five of us."

"Well, then, I will provide a feast for you and your friends. It will be a night to remember."

"Thank you." Hadley could barely contain her excitement. She couldn't wait to tell Luca her big news. She was bursting with happiness.

Gina led Hadley to her table. When Hadley told her the news, Gina wrapped her in her arms and wept. "Does Luca know?"

"I'm going to tell him tonight."

Gina put her hand to her heart. "That will make Mama Ferrari very happy."

Hadley laughed. That was an understatement. Gina went to a table in the rear of the restaurant and began a conversation with an elegantly dressed woman dining alone.

When Hadley saw Ingrid, Isabella, and Prince Vittorio arrive, she motioned them over.

She and Ingrid hugged.

"Let me see the ring," Hadley said, turning to Isabella.

Isabella looked beautiful, as always. She held out her ring finger, and Hadley was almost blinded by the sparkle of the stone.

"It's magnificent. I'm so happy for you." She and Isabella squealed and hugged.

"It is a family heirloom," said the prince. "But it pales in comparison to my Isabella's beauty." Vittorio was obviously besotted.

Isabella squeezed his hand. It was wonderful to see Isabella smile. They were so clearly in love.

"How's your father?" Hadley asked. She had worked with the prince's father in Lake Como to recover a long-lost Vermeer.

"He sends his regards and is looking forward to seeing you at the wedding."

"Have you set a date?" Hadley asked.

"As soon as possible," said the prince. "I am anxious for Isabella to become my wife." Isabella beamed.

"Where's Luca?" Ingrid asked.

"He's coming in from work. He should be here any minute. Let's sit down."

As if she had conjured him up, Luca walked in, looking as scrumptious as ever. He hugged Gina and strode on to their table.

Hadley moved over in the booth and made room for her husband while everyone greeted Luca. Hadley made the introductions to Isabella's fiancé. "Luca, this is

Sandro Rossi's son, Prince Vittorio. He and Isabella just got engaged."

Luca got up and kissed Isabella on the cheek. "That's wonderful." He turned to Prince Vittorio. "You are a lucky man." It wasn't too long ago that Hadley had been insanely jealous of Isabella and all the attention Luca was focusing on her. But even though Isabella was a beauty, Luca had chosen Hadley. He had only lavished attention on Isabella because she was vulnerable and needed protection. And Hadley knew her husband was all about coming to the rescue of anyone who needed him.

"I know it," said the prince, who signaled Gina and ordered champagne for the table.

Gina brought over a bottle and filled each champagne flute. A waiter brought out plates of appetizers, pasta, and risotto for the table to share. He kept the food coming, from salads and entrees to sides and desserts.

"Tonight, I have a big surprise," Gina announced. "There happens to be a special guest in our restaurant, an opera singer, and she's agreed to sing for us."

"Gina, that's wonderful," Hadley exclaimed.

Gina inclined her head toward a beautiful woman whose long dark hair blended into a flowing black midi dress as she strolled to her place next to the piano. Gina also headed toward the piano. Hadley knew the restaurant featured entertainers on weekends, but she didn't know Gina could play.

"You're a pianist, too?" Hadley inquired.

Gina winked. "On occasion. And this is a special occasion."

"Isn't that—?" asked Luca.

"Yes," replied Gina, smiling.

"How do you know her?"

"We were friends from Capri. She often dines here, and she loves to sing and entertain."

Luca was a singer himself, and he loved opera. At the station, they called him "The Voice." Hadley knew a lot about art, but she knew nothing about opera. Luca, on the other hand, sang in the shower, and he had a deep and powerful voice.

Gina stood at the piano. "I'd like to introduce a woman who really needs no introduction. We are very lucky she will sing for us this evening. You're all in for a special treat. She will start out with 'O Mio Babbino Caro,' a Puccini aria."

Gina sat at the piano and began to play, and when the soprano sang, the restaurant went silent. The beautiful tones coming out of her mouth were magnificent and brought Hadley to tears.

"What is she saying?" Hadley asked Luca, mesmerized.

"She is begging her father to help her marry her lover, and if she can't have him, she will throw herself in the Arno River," he whispered.

"How tragic."

"That is art," Luca stated, rising to his feet to clap thunderously when she finished.

The soprano sang two more arias in Italian and then, for the Americans in the room, sang some familiar songs from Broadway musicals, including "I Could Have Danced All Night," from *My Fair Lady.*

The diners could not stop applauding.

"Wait, where's that server?" Ingrid joked. "We haven't eaten in ten minutes."

"Let's have a toast to the happy couple—Isabella and Vittorio," Hadley announced. "May they have a life full of love."

Everyone at the table drained their glasses, but Luca noticed Hadley hadn't touched her drink.

"You're not drinking? This is a celebration."

Hadley shrugged, lifting her shoulders without an explanation.

"Is everything all right? Are you unhappy about something? Are you mad at me?"

The table was buzzing, so Luca leaned in and whispered to Hadley, "I have something to say. I've been thinking about this all day."

"About what?"

"I don't want to rush you about starting a family. I don't care what my mother says. I don't want to lose you. Your career comes first, and I am very proud of you. We can wait until the time is right to have babies. I don't want you to feel like you're under any pressure. I'm fine if we don't have children now."

Hadley blushed and whispered, "Don't you want this baby?"

"What are you talking about?"

"The baby. Our baby. I'm pregnant."

Luca turned to Hadley and wrapped her in his arms, whispering against her ear, "*Cara*, is it true?"

"Yes."

The big smile on Luca's face told Hadley everything she wanted to know.

"What should we call him?"

Hadley's eyebrows shot up. "How do you know it's going to be a him? What if it's a her?"

"It happened very quickly," he said, smiling. "I must

be very powerful."

"It was that night at the hotel in Rome. I'll admit, you have a lot of staying power."

"That's how I know it's going to be a boy."

"Girls can be powerful, too. I was thinking of calling her Fragonard."

Luca laughed. "That's a French name. Of course the name must be Italian. How about Fabio Ferrari?"

"Or Francesca Ferrari."

"No matter. You have made me very happy. Wait until Mama hears about this." Then Luca turned toward the others at the table.

"Everyone, my wife has just announced I am going to be a father. We're pregnant. That is, Hadley is pregnant. We are going to be a family."

Everyone at the table clapped.

"More champagne," said the prince. "Tonight is on me."

"This will be a night to remember," said Luca.

Hadley recalled all the frogs she'd had to kiss before she found her prince. The endless panel of suitors her parents had paraded in front of her to keep her in Tallahassee.

There was one memorable candidate in particular—Stanley Elgart—a freckle-faced boy with curly red hair, who majored in Creative Arts with a minor in Music Theatre. He had rented out an auditorium and invited her to a multimedia performing arts program. It was a stage art performance she'd tried to forget but couldn't unsee.

As the curtains rose, the spotlight followed the brillo-headed Stanley dancing across the stage and singing, with a side of acrobatics, followed by a self-narrated PowerPoint about his life—in case she was interested, which she definitely was not. At the end, he handed Hadley a four-color brochure about his attributes and a freshly-printed business card. She said the only thing she could think of at the time. "You're very...flexible...and your presentation was very professional and informative."

"Everyone's a critic," he'd mumbled, realizing his antics hadn't hit the mark. After which they parted ways as quickly as possible but not before he asked, if she wasn't interested, could she recommend some of her friends who might be. He handed her some extra cards, just in case.

Then there was her long-term relationship with King Charles, otherwise known as Charles King. Suffice it to say, her romance with Luca had a happier ending. She was exactly where she wanted to be and with whom she wanted to be.

Hadley leaned into Luca, and he wound his arm protectively around her shoulders.

"I love you, *cara*," he said.

"And I love you, more than I can say."

A word about the author…

Marilyn Baron is a public relations consultant in Atlanta. She's a member of Atlanta Writers Club and Georgia Romance Writers. She writes in a variety of genres, from Women's Fiction to Historical Romantic Thrillers and Romantic Suspense to Cozy Mysteries and has won writing awards in single title, suspense romance, novel with strong romantic elements, and paranormal/fantasy romance. She was the Finalist in the 2017 Georgia Author of the Year (GAYA) Award in the Romance category for her novel *Stumble Stones* and the Finalist for the 2018 GAYA Awards in the Romance category for her novel *The Alibi*. Her new book, *The Case of the Forgotten Fragonard*, is her 28th work of fiction. She was past chair of Roswell Reads and serves on the Atlanta Author Series Steering Committee.

She graduated from the University of Florida in Gainesville, Florida, with a Bachelor of Science in Journalism (Public Relations sequence) and a minor in Creative Writing. Born in Miami, Florida, Marilyn lives in Atlanta, Georgia, with her husband. They have two daughters and two granddaughters.

She says: "What's unique about my writing? I try to inject humor into everything I write. I like to laugh and my readers do too. I love to travel and often set my books in places I've visited. My favorite place to visit is Italy because I studied in Florence for six months in my junior year of college."

To find out more about Marilyn's books, please visit her website at www.marilynbaron.com.

Thank you for purchasing
this publication of The Wild Rose Press, Inc.

For questions or more information
contact us at
info@thewildrosepress.com.

The Wild Rose Press, Inc.